COPS HELPLESS!
CITY PARALYZED WITH FEAR!
Behavior of Rat in Cage
Predicts Killer's Next Move.

Yes, these could be tomorrow's headlines in today's overpopulated world. Leonard Simon has created a frightening and all-too-plausible thriller that pits an experimental psychologist, his liberated girlfriend, and a group of ghetto youths with records as long as your arm—against an All-American clean-cut killer with a rat's eye view of the human condition.

THE IRVING SOLUTION chillingly parallels the plight of men in the city and rats in the laboratory when overcrowding drives the struggle for existence to a frenzied pitch—and a new breed murders in the service of survival.

One warning: you've heard of New York City's subway. After experiencing the harrowing climax of this novel, you won't go down there without feeling a strange tingle of fear.

"TOTALLY CONVINCING . . .
RAISES INTELLIGENT QUESTIONS."
Publishers Weekly

"GRIPPING . . . HORRIFYING"
Booklist

THE IRVING SOLUTION

LEONARD SIMON

AVON
PUBLISHERS OF BARD, CAMELOT AND DISCUS BOOKS

AVON BOOKS
A division of
The Hearst Corporation
959 Eighth Avenue
New York, New York 10019

Copyright © 1977 by Leonard Simon
Published by arrangement with Arbor House Publishing Co., ınc.
Library of Congress Catalog Card Number: 76-39719
ISBN: 0-380-01928-0

First Avon Printing, March, 1978

AVON TRADEMARK REG. U.S. PAT. OFF. AND IN
OTHER COUNTRIES, MARCA REGISTRADA, HECHO EN
U.S.A.

Printed in the U.S.A.

Basically, then, there are only two kinds of solutions to the population problem. One is a "birth rate solution," in which we find ways to lower the birth rate. The other is a "death rate solution," in which ways to raise the death rate—war, famine, pestilence—*find us*.

Paul R. Ehrlich

· 1 ·

IN THE BOWELS of the city a man conducts an experiment. Locked in a basement laboratory, beneath a well-known college, he patiently observes the·ebb and flow of life within a giant box that holds a colony of rats. Oblivious, by choice, to everything around him, he tries to fill his consciousness with all that happens in that special world. He watches the births and deaths, the copulations and assaults within the colony. He sees it all and feels it all within himself and hopes, out of the experience, to make something he would call Science. He hopes to understand it so profoundly that he may come up with something new and valuable to say: a new theory, a new set of observations, a way to explain the peculiar and destructive manner in which these animals behave.

The man also knows, without saying it, without ever telling himself about it, that his work is more than abstract science. In some peculiar way it connects with his life. It touches a part of him that is, like the behavior of his animals, still uncharted territory. He has built their world, molded their lives, explored their eccentricities, counted their dead. Every step along the way is filled with fear and fascination. This is no detached investigation of abnormal animals; at least equally it is a study of himself.

·2·

THE FIRST TO DIE were very poor. It was the reason, perhaps, their deaths were hardly noticed.

On West 128th Street, in Harlem, in her furnished room, Mrs. Ethel Davis, a widow, sixty-eight years old, died in her sleep. Her body was found the next morning, after she failed to appear in church, and the neighbors assumed that her time had just come quickly. She must have had a stroke, they said, or a heart attack; she had been telling them for years that her blood pressure was too high.

Five blocks away Mrs. Angela Martinez, age sixty, also a widow, also died in her sleep. Her body was found by her grandson, Jesus, who called an aunt from the candy store downstairs after he searched the apartment. He found the twenty-dollar bill she kept in her Bible and her gold earrings, a wedding present from her mother, which he would take to the hockshop after he had his fix. He's run out of money the day before and had visited the old lady in the hope of stealing something. The chills and nausea he was beginning to feel were just a taste of what would happen if he couldn't make a connection.

Less than a mile to the south, on 108th Street, Samuel Greenberg, eighty years old, was also dead, but no one knew it yet, nor would they for the next two days, when his body would begin to call attention to itself. With the exception of his social worker, Samuel Greenberg was never visited by anyone. He was simply a silent face in a second floor window, one of thousands in the city, lucky that he was not yet jammed into a nursing home, but only slightly better off. No one noticed that he only left his room on the day they distributed surplus food at the welfare center. No one helped him drag his shopping cart outside for the slow, agonizing walk uptown.

Arthur Washington died more spectacularly. He was fifty-five years old, a heavy drinker, with recently diagnosed severe diabetes. He was sitting on the stoop and talking with the men, bragging about his new woman, the good food and care and lovin' that big fat mama gave him. He was hit by a wave of nausea. He knew he shouldn't have been drinking and he blamed his discomfort on the quart of muscatel he had just put away. When the nausea came again he retched in the street. Except for his embarrassment he felt much better. But then, quite suddenly, he collapsed on the pavement, went into convulsions, and died long before the ambulance—which took its time in coming—arrived. And the young white intern in his starched white uniform felt the hostile eyes of a hundred silent onlookers as he examined the black man and pronounced him dead.

In Riverside Park at 110th Street Mrs. Maria Torres walked slowly, hand in hand with her two oldest children. Their dinner eaten, they were out for a stroll beside the murky Hudson. The air was almost unbreathable; hot, damp, and foul-smelling, permeated with the stench of automobiles from the heavy traffic on the West Side Drive, but still an improvement over what passed for air in their hot and cramped apartment, where the baby cried incessantly and where it was crying, alone, at that moment. Then Ramon, her three-year-old, complained that he felt cold. He began to shiver violently, and she wrapped her arms around his thin body, lifted him off the ground, and softly promised him that soon they would be home. Carmen, her four-year-old, also began to complain but Maria thought she was just copying the boy, jealous as usual, and she hushed the child abruptly. Then she felt chilled herself. They must all have a fever, she decided. She tried to walk more quickly, to get them home and into bed, but her legs grew heavier with every step. Soon she had to rest on a bench. She was certain she would fall if she tried to walk on. She held the children against her body and waited for her strength to return. For a while the little ones whimpered, confused and uncomfortable, but then they grew silent. She tried to get someone to help, but no one would stop. They assumed she was an addict. Someone made the comment that her children should be taken away. She began to cry. In a little while she lay down on the bench. A breeze lifted her skirt provocatively, but she was unable to move. And they were all still there, long after dark, when a passing policeman attempted to wake them, prodding Mrs. Torres in the breast with his nightstick and then shaking her shoulder. It was obvious then that all three of them were dead.

Mary Dubovick believed she had the flu. She complained of how sick she felt when her caseworker arrived. She needed help with the children, she said, they were just too much to handle when she felt this bad. They were driving her up the wall. She knew she was entitled to a homemaker; if she had to take much more she'd go back on drugs. Surprisingly, the bitch agreed to help. She went further than Mary expected or desired. She insisted on a visit to the clinic. She would watch the children herself until she could arrange for someone.

Mary was forced to play along. It was more than she had bargained for. The jerks that worked for Welfare now were capable of anything. She would go out for a little drink and tell the girl they sent her home. She wouldn't spend the day at a stupid clinic; having to go to one for her methadone was enough of a drag. But when she reached the street she felt much worse, and despite her belief—widespread in the neighborhood—that the place was a slaughterhouse, she took a cab to West Side Hospital. She began to shiver in the car and lose control of her body. She told the driver to skip the clinic and take her to the emergency room. With his help she made it through the door before collapsing. Under normal circumstances it is almost certain that she would have died right there; assumed, as had been true enough in the past, to be the victim of an overdose of heroin. But the hospital staff was now aware that something new was killing people. They placed her under special observation. Before she died they saw the tremors that racked her arms and legs, her breathing difficulties, and then the convulsions. It was nothing like an overdose at all.

Later that afternoon the young caseworker, unable to convince the appropriate city agency that there was a justifiable need for a homemaker, waited with increasing impatience for Mary to return. The kids had worn her out. She could see how hard life really was for the woman. Now at least they were quiet in front of the television set. She tried calling the clinic and was eventually, after an interminable wait, connected with the emergency room. She was stunned at what they told her, but able to function in the crisis. Her supervisor would approve. There were no relatives, so a children's shelter would have to be called. She would make the arrangements first and then tell the children. Perhaps she could have them all placed together. But just as she began to dial the telephone the oldest boy crept into the kitchen. He fell on his face and his body began to shake. She called the hospital again, and they responded quickly, but it was no use. By morning, along with a dozen more in the area, old and young and in between, all six Dubovick children were dead.

· 3 ·

SOLOMON GOLDENSON was immersed in his work. He had been in the basement laboratory of the college for three solid days and nights, sleeping on his cot when he needed it, and he expected to remain there, with only occasional excursions outside, for at least a month and perhaps much more. He had no awareness of what was happening in the streets above his lab, of the death and turmoil in the city. He had lost all track of time, and though he knew from the clock on the wall that it was three, he would have been unable to say for sure whether it was morning or afternoon without examining his notes. The laboratory was windowless, deep beneath the city, almost as far down as the subways, and he could sometimes feel the vibration and hear the rumble of the trains that passed beneath him. It was the only sound of the outside world that ever intruded, and yet it troubled him when it did.

Goldenson sat beside the huge wooden enclosure that housed the colony of rats that he was studying. He peered in at his animals through a small window, one of several on each wall. His beard was scraggly, his hair uncombed, and he was wearing jeans, tennis shoes, and an old Harvard sweat shirt. He appeared fully absorbed in his observation of the animals. On his head was a pair of earphones. From time to time he made notes on a clipboard on his lap, and once he pushed a button on a control panel beside a window. There was nothing in his behavior to distinguish him from a conventional scientist, and perhaps his appearance could have been explained by the fact that he spent almost all his time in the exclusive company of a large colony of rats. But there was one striking and peculiar feature: the way his body rocked as he watched, the way his head bobbed back and forth, as if he was performing a kind of stationary dance. One might have thought it helped him concentrate. Perhaps it prevented his muscles from becoming stiff. After a while one noticed that the cable to the earphones had no connection with the enclosure. It led instead to an amplifier and record changer on the far side of the room. And the last record on the stack, a Bartok string quartet, was almost over when a tall thin black man came through the door and placed both hands on his back.

Goldenson leaped and turned in a graceful movement he had obviously learned in a karate class. He showed no fear. He looked up at the clock, removed his earphones, and extended his hand to the visitor, Ed Hall, his part-time laboratory assistant.

"Your timing's off," Hall said. "You must be uptight."

"You would be too if you saw what's happening in there."

The black man glanced at the enclosure and restrained his urge to look inside. "It was a nice idea," he said. "We did good work on it."

"It's still a nice idea," said Goldenson. "No matter what they do to each other."

"I don't mean that," said Hall. "Don't you listen to anything beside that weird music?"

"Like what?"

"Like the radio."

"Not for days." It began to dawn on Goldenson that something apparently had happened outside. "Who did they assassinate this time?" he asked.

"No one special," said Hall. He revealed a bitter smile and perfect teeth. "Only twenty-one niggers dead. About a dozen white folks too."

"Oh God, man," said Goldenson. He was visibly upset. "How? Where?"

"They were killed like roaches," Hall went on, "and Harlem is the nest. The city is going wild. There's panic everywhere.

You can't walk the streets without running into some psychotic, without hearing some psychotic theory."

Goldenson turned a switch on his stereo system and the voice of a black announcer came over the loudspeaker. The next news report would follow soon; in the interval they would play appropriate music. A gospel group began to sing. Instead of tuning in another station he poured coffee for himself and Hall. "What else can you tell me?" he asked.

"Just one more thing: get your white ass out of here. I came to make sure of that. By tomorrow night there will be war. Nothing can stop it now. It was bound to happen anyway, sooner or later. We all knew it. It was only a question of time. Harlem or South Africa, it doesn't matter."

Goldenson sipped his coffee. His mind was working rapidly. When Hall remained standing he spoke to him in anger: "Oh come on, man, will you stop playing revolutionary. Those days are over. Will you sit yourself down here and look me in the face. Maybe I could do something."

"Don't be ridiculous, just get out of here. This is not a college game. This is not college politics. This is not politics of any sort. There are no dumb liberals here for you to hassle. There's nothing you can do, no animals to play with, no hypotheses to test. You're detached, man. Your thing is elsewhere. You're out of it, just what you always wanted. Walk the wrong street tonight, walk any street and you'll be dead, I don't care how much of a radical you once pretended to be."

"Even if you were with me?" Goldenson ignored the insults.

"We'd both be dead." Hall closed his eyes and swayed slightly. He seemed to want to sit, even to fall, but somehow he found the strength to maintain his stance. "Don't you understand . . . the feeling now is different. The city has gone mad. Everyone is ready to kill everyone else. It's like a war has started. Nothing white is gonna live in Harlem." He looked more and more unhappy as he stood there silently. "At least not in this college," he said at last, "that's for sure."

"Meaning what?" Goldenson asked. It was the first time he felt that he personally had something to fear.

"You know what this place stands for. You know as well as anyone. You know the way the people hate it. When we tried to change it, when we played their dirty game, they showed how dumb and powerless we were. They let us make our noise and then ignored us. When the city ran low on cash they kicked us out as soon as possible. But that's all over now. By tomorrow night there'll be no college. They're going to burn it down. There's a rumor going round that whoever caused this thing works here."

"Who's saying that?"

"The kids I work with. They've been all over town. They're saying it, and kids in other gangs are saying it, and nothing I tell them is worth a damn."

"And when are they planning to come here?"

"I want you to leave right now."

"Are you nuts? I have my animals—"

"Tomorrow you won't get out." Hall paced the floor. "Listen, man, this is happening. If you don't go now, you won't get out. Tomorrow will be madness. The whites will throw a wall around us, or at least they'll try."

"Like that one?" asked Goldenson. He pointed at the enclosure.

"Maybe," said Hall. His mood changed rapidly to sadness. He was certain it would all end horribly, and equally certain that nothing could stop a conflagration. "But we won't do as well as them. We won't have you to bring us food and water."

"I'd try," said Goldenson. Then he paused and spoke intensely: "I can't leave. There's too much work in this. You know what was involved. If I went now, it would put me back a whole year. The animals would die. I'd have to start all over."

"Man, fuck your dissertation. Don't you understand? If you don't get out of here your life is over." Hall was almost pleading. "These kids are going wild. I can't control them. I have no way of stopping them. They don't give a damn about anything I say."

"I'll take my chances. Maybe they won't bother with the basement."

"A rat in his hole." Hall touched Goldenson on the shoulder. "The basement won't protect you. You'll burn with your fucking rats. I'll be lucky if they don't burn me."

"I'll wait a day," said Goldenson. "I'll listen to the radio. If it looks that bad I'll leave tomorrow. I wish you luck. I hope you

15

can talk some sense into them. Protect that woolly head of yours."

"I'll check back if I get the chance. Don't count on anything."

They walked together to the door. "I know the spot you're in," said Goldenson. He touched Hall's arm. "I appreciate your coming."

"There are limits to everything," said Hall, "especially now. I don't know what I can do. I'm in between, but if I have to choose there's only one way I can go."

"A false dichotomy," said Goldenson, but by the time he said it Hall was already gone.

· 4 ·

IT WAS LIKE the mysterious fever that had struck not so long before in Philadelphia. No one could find the cause. Laboratories all over the city were working frantically. Autopsies were performed on every suspicious body. Chemical analyses of hearts, livers, lungs, and other organs were all in progress. Teams of experts descended on the city. The newspapers speculated on the cause; their medical reporters had a field day with theories that ranged from one claiming a toxic reaction to the recent heavy air pollution—there had been high concentrations of lead, mercury, zinc, cadmium, and other substances in the air that week—to another that expressed the view that a new contaminant was in the city's water, possibly nickel, less visible than the small white worms that recently emerged from faucets in one neighborhood, but far more deadly. The New York *Post* ran the headline, BLACK DEATH!! and presented an interview with an unknown biologist who claimed that the world was ripe for a new outbreak of bubonic plague.

It was just good luck that Dr. Hilton Brown, newly arrived from North Carolina for a residency in obstetrics, was present in the emergency room when the Dubovick children were carried in. He guessed almost at once that they had been killed by an insecticide. He had seen dozens of such cases when he worked around the tobacco fields. And there was amazement in the hospital when, three hours later, word came down from the laboratory that he was right. The cause of death was a chemical called parathion. Since DDT was banned it had become the most widely used and deadly insecticide in the world. He had saved the lab at least a day and established a diagnostic reputation that would last throughout his life. But there was no reason for surprise; the diagnosis would have occurred to any physician who had ever treated farm workers. It was just that in New York they had different problems. If he had had to deal then with a heroin overdose or a case of lead poisoning, he would have been just as confused as they had been by an agricultural chemical in Harlem.

The police knew what to look for now. Perhaps they should have suspected sooner, but they had been unable to distinguish between those who died conventional deaths and those who had been poisoned. The only food in the Dubovick apartment was a sack of rice, a loaf of white bread, a jar of peanut butter and some cans of Coke and beer. The only food in the Torres apartment was an identical sack of rice and a smaller one of dried beans. There were cans of evaporated milk for the Torres baby, and it was still alive. Samuel Greenberg had lived—and died—on rice. It came just two days ago, from the welfare center on 125th Street. Several hundred identical sacks had been distributed and the center still had another fifty on hand. Samples were brought at once to the laboratory. In an hour they knew that all the rice was heavily contaminated. It had happened before: eighty-one people once in South America, seventeen at one time in Mexico, but never before in New York, and no one in the police department had ever seen a death caused by parathion.

There was no alternative to publicity. They had to do what they could to keep people from eating the rice. The word went out on television, on the radio, and in the newspapers. The announcers were uniformly calm. The similarity to prior occurrences of food poisoning was pointed out, to old incidents of mercury in tuna and swordfish and botulism in vichysoisse. Everyone emphasized that it all was a horrible accident; just an awful, horrible accident. But no words, no platitudes could change the fact that it had happened in Harlem, that the victims were mostly black and Puerto Rican, and that all were very poor.

The news spread quickly. Predictably, it was met at first with fear, and then with random, mindless rage. Almost everyone on the streets came to believe it was premeditated: the intentional elimination of the poor. The prediction made for so many years by so many different people, that the rich and white would one day try to kill them all, seemed at last to be coming true. It had happened in South Africa, why not New York? Within an hour after the news was announced two welfare centers were attacked with firebombs. Within two hours large crowds had formed on major streets, especially outside of the welfare center on 125th Street. The people stood together in small groups within the larger mass, still numb with what was happening, listening to each other talk, not yet sure in which way they were going to move. There were those who believed that the end was at hand and that all should kneel together in the streets and pray, but there were more who argued that murder should be met with greater murder, and more still who said nothing at all but simply looked up and down the street for the liquor stores and other convenient targets.

Soon cars were stopped, turned over, and burned on all the major streets of Harlem. Their white occupants were beaten, then driven off, one dying of a heart attack, eight stomped to death, four stabbed, all losing their wallets in the process. The police made several unsuccessful attempts to disperse the largest crowd, which was still growing. They exercised extreme restraint, keeping all their elaborate riot equipment well concealed. They made no show of force, nor did they seem yet in a position to do so. The situation was more ominous than it had ever been in any city in the United States. There were already voices urging people to attack outside the ghetto. Isolated individuals lit fires in two major midtown department stores. A smoke bomb was set off in Grand Central Station where thousands of commuters were trapped as train service through upper Manhattan halted, the result of at least one sniper and a deluge of debris from the bridges that crossed the tracks.

It soon became clear that the only hope—if there was still any hope—lay in dramatic action, and the mayor, whose popularity had reached a new low even for mayors of New York, was brave enough to take it. He boarded a police helicopter and was flown to the roof of the welfare center. A team of black aides had been brought in earlier to set up loudspeakers, and a mobile TV unit with an all-black crew had managed to penetrate the crowd. The light was beginning to fail, but the image that appeared on the television screen was of excellent quality. The mayor stood there alone, on the roof of the low building, his clothes rumpled, his skin a ghostly white, his hands shaking as if he had been poisoned himself. He made no attempt to conceal his emotion, but his voice, trembling slightly, remained under control: "I believe that in some way I can understand your agony." There was a hush, then a yell of derision from a man up front. The mayor looked startled, but he went on: "Only in a small way, I grant you that, for though I am a brother, I am not a black man or a Puerto Rican." He paused again. "But I am a man, I am a human being, and I feel deeply, more deeply than I can possibly convey, the tragedy of what has occurred in our city today. We are all in this together. I know what some believe, and I repeat to you, this is not racial. Whites have been killed too. This is a sad and terrible accident, and those who call it racial, those who call it genocide, are spitting on the graves of those now dead."

A man screamed out, "You spit with every lying word."

The mayor went on with more bitterness in his voice: "They are using the dead for their own foul purposes and they would plunge us deep into a horror from which there is no return. If genocide had been the aim of the white community it would have been done long, long ago and far more effectively than this—"

The man began to yell again. "It has been done, it has been done." The people around him all agreed.

The mayor shifted to another point. "Give us the chance to find the facts. Whoever is responsible for these killings will be found. He will be identified and punished. The dead will not go unmourned or unrevenged." He paused, and the crowd became silent. They had liked this man once, though in fact he had done little for them. Perhaps the best that could be said was that he harmed them less than the others. "I give you my word, I swear to you. The person responsible will be found. No matter what his office is, no matter who he is, he will be found and punished. I give you my word." He looked down at the crowd. "And now I beg you to leave the streets. There has been enough death and agony today. I urge you to return to your homes. Do not turn your rage—your justifiable rage—on your own community. Consider the possibility that we have *all* been manipulated. Consider the possibility that whoever caused these deaths was seeking to provoke a race war." Now he raised his voice: "Let's find out, and let's punish those responsible. Please give us this chance before we are all destroyed." He looked down at the crowd again and whispered, "Go home. I beg you, go home."

The people finally did. It was without a doubt the mayor's most effective moment, the high point of his career. He would continue downhill after this, but this moment would justify all his years of relative ineffectuality. The immediate danger was averted. The mass of people left the streets, returned to their television sets, and Harlem was to be more peaceful that night than anyone would have imagined possible.

But the forces already in motion could hardly be contained by any speech.

· 5 ·

Now Wendy McGhie was pounding on Goldenson's heavy door. He had locked it securely after Ed Hall's visit and she was forced to rap her sandal on the thick steel for a full five minutes until, at a quiet moment, he could hear her vibrations above those of the Stravinsky piece he had been listening to.

"They're running like rats," she said casually. "The whole damn place is in a panic. Everyone in the college wants out of Harlem."

"I can't talk now," he said on his way back to the enclosure. She dumped her books on his desk and slowly circled the room. There was another record on the changer, and she knew he would be at work until it was over; he arranged the music to fit his schedule of observation. She flipped a switch on the amplifier and the loud, insistent music filled the room. She studied the back of his head, frowned, then switched it off. Then she picked up one of her books and began to read, turning the pages quickly and walking all the while in rapid circles. Wendy was a plump, strikingly attractive young woman. She had large breasts that jiggled with every move she made and were clearly, even dramatically visible beneath her sweater. She wore no bra, and her erect nipples stood out assertively, like the toughness in her Irish face, defiant, yet barely concealing the softness beneath. At the right provocation she was capable of letting loose a string of curses that might span the centuries—from Old to Middle to contemporary English—and she could seriously confuse, if not render impotent, even the most articulate and obscene construction worker. It was one of the few reasons she was thankful she had once been an English major. Now she was studying history, emphasis on the role of women.

"Calhoun really found something," said Goldenson as he removed his earphones and crossed the room. Calhoun was the biologist who had originated the line of research that he was following. "Not that I doubted him, I like his style too much for that, but it's nice to see it working out. With every week things get a little more bizarre. We're really approaching something critical." He counted a set of marks on his clipboard, wrote the total on the bottom of the page, then stepped across the laboratory to a large blackboard that dominated one wall. He checked his coordinates and carefully placed a mark on the board. Then he drew a rising line that connected an older mark with the one he had just drawn. Whatever he was tallying had taken an upward jump.

He turned back to Wendy, placed his hands on her shoulders and kissed her forehead. "Do you want some wine?" She nodded and he opened the refrigerator. Next to the bottle of chablis, in numbered plastic bags, was a pile of rat carcasses awaiting autopsy. He poured, and she sipped, blissfully unaware of the wine's recent neighbors. Anyway, it tasted fine.

"Now tell me what else is happening." He stretched, made a few karate movements, then massaged the back of his neck. His muscles were stiff from the hours at the observation window. "What's the latest disaster?"

"The latest disaster is that I had to leave the library. I was in the middle of birth control in the fifteenth century—it's a fact—when the idiots began to panic about rampaging blacks. Nothing new happened. I assume you know the story. Nothing is *going* to happen. The mayor rose brilliantly to the occasion. His rhetoric was at last appropriate. People went home to watch the tube and maybe see themselves in the crowd. What can they do? What hope do they have? They're fish in a barrel, and they know it better than we do."

"According to Ed Hall, the barrel has a leak."

"I'll believe it when I see it."

"He tried to get me to leave. He predicts an attack on the college tomorrow."

"So does everyone else," she said. "Even the head librarian. That's another reason why it'll never happen."

"Anyway," said Goldenson, "I told him I would hang around. I'm too much into this to leave right now."

"I thought I'd stay the night," she said.

He looked intently into her eyes. "You're a crazy lady," he said softly. "It *could* be dangerous. And I have another hour of work."

"I brought my books," she said, slightly annoyed. "I can amuse myself. I didn't just come to screw."

He prepared an omelette on his hot plate and they ate together on a small table she cleared and set. She complimented his cooking, and together they finished the bottle of wine. Though neither believed that they were in any serious danger, the feeling between them was charged by the tension in the city. The radio reported that Harlem was still calm, though now there had been firebomb attacks on a bank and an office building in the suburbs. No more whites were hurt, and no residences attacked, but defense committees had sprung up everywhere and local blacks, even elderly maids, were being driven from the streets. "If we have anyone to fear," Goldenson said, "it's the rednecks."

It was not that Wendy and Goldenson were especially brave or especially indifferent to violence. It was just that years of one crisis after another had made them casual about the wild predictions of people caught in the middle of things, as Ed Hall was, and about the distortions and exaggerations of the media. They knew enough to make the most of the time they had together, to ignore the panic of the people around them.

Goldenson sipped his wine and talked about his experiment. It was, for him, a pleasant evening with a woman he cared about after a day of work that absorbed him. Perhaps the meal was tinged with sadness at the deaths, perhaps he could taste the possibility of danger, but still it was a time when he could do almost whatever he pleased, live almost the way he chose. He had elected a kind of freedom; to live in a world that barely touched, he told himself, the rest of the country. And though he knew better—once, long ago, he had been politically active and Wendy now still was—he pretended to himself that he could escape the agonies of that larger world. Like many of his generation, he had grown tired of politics, worn out by constant crises. He was involved in ideas now, in his own research, not so different from the way people in universities used to be.

They sat there together until it was time for Goldenson to work again. His skin had a healthy glow about it now, his face a kind of joy. He arranged another stack of records on the turntable. The music was Mozart now, the G-minor Quintet; and Wendy smiled as she heard the opening bars. It was just the right choice, exactly the right feeling. At last he seated himself beside the enclosure and began, once more, to peer inside.

· 6 ·

GOLDENSON'S ANIMALS were housed in a huge wooden box, fifteen feet square and seven feet high, that he and Ed Hall had built together many months ago. Its plan was an adaptation of one described by the biologist John Calhoun, but it was considerably larger and it contained many more animals than ever had been used in prior experiments. It sat there in the basement, dominating one side of the room, an environment designed for the study of crowding in a colony of rats. Almost self-contained, it existed as a kind of space capsule in the middle of the lab; a special world, a special planet. It had its own electrical system and its own air conditioner. It required a person only to provide a supply of food and water and remove the droppings that accumulated and what little was uneaten of those animals that died. Most of these functions could easily have been automated, but Goldenson performed them himself. He felt that daily visits inside the enclosure, though highly upsetting to him, helped his understanding of the life in there. But his real task, the reason it had all been arranged, was just to observe, to sit outside the box and watch what happened to creatures forced to live and reproduce within those walls, within that teeming, seething pot of life.

On the inside the enclosure was swarming with albino rats, well over four hundred adults at last count, and the population was still increasing, though now the rate was leveling off. It was an insane environment for any living creature, more overcrowded than any that could exist in nature, at least the way nature was before man began to tamper with it. And yet these animals were able to adapt and show a special intelligence in the ways they stayed alive. That in itself was a paradox; that these white creatures with their grotesque pink eyes, insipid imitations of rats that existed in the real world, could manage to survive. They were a pure strain of albino rats, bred for several hundred generations for a single absurd fate: to be used in a laboratory experiment. Living blobs of flesh and fur created for the convenience of someone who believed in science. A genetically consistent lump, as similar as possible from one litter to the next, so that scientists would know that their results could be compared.

Not that results obtained on animals like these would be the same as those for rats that had lived in the world. Somewhere along the way, as the laboratory strain evolved, it had turned into something new. Though these animals were genetically still rats, could still have interbred with the larger and darker and hipper rats of Harlem, they could never have survived unaided in the world outside. It was not just that they were born and raised in the protected environment of a laboratory. That would limit the potential of any animal. More important was the fact that they carried genes that had prevailed over all those generations to produce a creature suited best for life inside a cage. They could have been called stupid in comparison with wild rats; less vigorous in their movements, less intense in their responses, less sensitive to stimulation, more stereotyped in the way they behaved. There was only one dimension on which they exceeded normal rats—their sociability, their docile, amiable, lethargic ability to get along with their fellows in a community cage. They had been created for the laboratory, by the laboratory, and were ideally suited for the life and death that was inevitable for them within the laboratory. As the city created the people who inhabited it, so the laboratory had created these animals.

On the inside of the enclosure was a central open space in which a feeding trough was located. It was covered with a wire screen that interfered with the animal's access to food. The screen did not prevent the rats from obtaining all they wished to eat, but it slowed the process. During the time it was eating, each animal was compelled to stand beside the other animals around the trough. The rats were forced to engage in much more social contact than would ever have been their choice in nature. They were forced to interact with large numbers of other animals during the acts of eating, copulating, nest building, nursing and all the other activities that made up their lives. The research originated by Calhoun had examined some of the destructive effects of life in such an environment, and Goldenson, in his experiment, was extending the work.

The walls of the enclosure were lined with shelves on which the animals could nest, and several feet from each of the four corners were platforms that contained additional nesting space. The shelves and platforms were all connected by an intricate series of ramps, permitting the rats to wander around the enclosure without touching the floor. In contrast with Calhoun's original experiment and with real life—at least current life—the animals in Goldenson's enclosure had to conduct all their activities in the open, where he could observe and film them, and where the amount of social interaction was inevitably increased.

It was the extreme effects of this environment that Goldenson was studying. Not that the consequences were unknown—Calhoun had already described, in the early sixties, the behavorial aberrations that developed after only a few months of such a life, as well as its consequences on various aspects of the animal's physiology. And Goldenson had already observed the same developments. But Calhoun had stopped, at least in his published reports, at the point where things seemed to stabilize, and Goldenson was investigating what would happen if the community continued for a much longer period, and if the condition of crowding was made even more bizarre. He thought something new might emerge, a creative adaptation to the conditions under which the rats were forced to live—an evolutionary leap.

Now he watched, the Mozart in his ears, as a large female, heavy with a litter, edged slowly to the water tray. She seemed about to drink, but she stopped as her abdomen contracted visibly. He pressed the button to activate the movie camera; it was clear that she would soon deliver. The rat began to circle the area slowly. Normally she would have, long before, carefully prepared a nest, but under these conditions nest building almost never took place. Now she made her way to a far corner of the enclosure, and Goldenson activated a second camera. Next the rat found several shreds of paper, which she drew together with her front paws in a belated effort to construct a nest. Before she could make much progress the first pup of her litter began to emerge. He could see that it was alive, something that was becoming less and less frequent as the metabolic dysfunctions in the adult animals increased. Then the pup dropped free, and she cleaned it rapidly and waited for the second to be born, the attempt to build a nest abandoned.

Now another rat, apparently a male, approached the female and engaged in several abrupt fragments of a mating ritual. It was, again, behavior that would never have taken place in a normal environment. She bared her teeth and chased him off, but in the process moved several feet from her newborn pup. It was there that she had another contraction. When the second pup was born she cleaned it rapidly, lifted it by the neck, and attempted to carry it to the vicinity of the first. Before she covered half the distance two other rats approached and began to sniff at her. She dropped the pup and returned their gesture. Then she lifted the pup again, but before she could move on there was another set of contractions and the third pup of her litter was born. She dropped the second pup as she cleaned the third. Meanwhile, another rat was sniffing at her first. Now she left the second two and chased the intruder from the first of her pups. She lifted it in her jaws and carried it to the place where she had left the others. She licked each of the pups in turn as she sprawled beside them on the feces-covered floor. It was almost a happy home, except it could never last. Then, with another contraction, the fourth and last pup was born. She cleaned it and sprawled again, the four pups now rooting in her abdomen. She looked almost content as she lay there and nursed them, though Goldenson knew, as he watched and filmed the scene, that none of the pups could possibly survive. She had done a masterful job, but sooner or later she would become distracted. Conditions out there on the floor were too chaotic. There was just too much going on, too much social stimulation, too many sexual assaults. Sooner or later she would lose them. It was impossible for such a unit to remain together. If they did manage to survive, the pups would wander off before they could care for themselves. They would die of hunger, or be killed and eaten by larger rats. By that time she would be pregnant with another litter and the cycle would begin again. She would function as well as possible under the circumstances, but the circumstances would destroy her.

Goldenson had observed, as Calhoun had before him, the incredible alterations in maternal behavior that took place under these conditions. Rats were usually fantastically successful at protecting their young. But the only place, now, in which the young could survive—and even there the death rate was very high—was on the shelves around the enclosure. There it was still possible for a litter to remain intact, and it was the offspring of the females that were lucky enough or clever enough to deliver in these areas that kept the population expanding. Goldenson wondered whether these rats, the offspring of parents who had adapted most successfully, would themselves compete and reproduce. Would it be possible, if he kept things going long enough, to create a strain that would be suited for the life in the enclosure? It might be possible to study the effect of overpopulation on the genetic characteristics of his animals. The gene pool would eventually change. Then he wondered what would happen if he placed one of the new breed in a normal environment. That had all sorts of implications.

But now Goldenson stopped. He was finished until tomorrow, and happy to turn back in Wendy's direction. There was something about the experience of caring for and studying these animals that became incredibly wearing. It went far beyond the reality of what he had to do. He tried to be objective—to avoid endowing them with human qualities they couldn't possibly have—but there was still something that drew him into thinking of them as analogous to people. It was not an experiment in which some isolated behavior or organ system was under observation and one could avoid thinking about the whole animal. A rat—even a rat, even these rats—was more than just a convenient biological machine. He was watching the life cycle of a complete organism, an organism not that different from a human, living in conditions that were not that different either. They were being born, they were copulating and reproducing, and they were dying in a variety of natural and unnatural ways, also like humans. But he had to fight the tendency to anthropomorphize. It was too depressing, and more important, it would make it impossible to think clearly about his own results. It was also something his dissertation committee would never tolerate.

"Are you okay?" asked Wendy, as he stepped back from the window and rubbed his eyes.

"Yes," he said. "I should have called you. I watched a birth. The beginning of a new disaster. You would have been interested."

"I'm still studying the old disasters."

"It was incredible," he said. "She had her litter in the middle of the floor. They'll all be dead by morning. They don't have a chance out there."

He took a seat beside Wendy and poured himself a cup of the coffee she had made. Then he turned a news program on the radio. The announcer spoke:

"The fear that has gripped New York City and its suburbs eased somewhat this evening as anticipated riots by welfare recipients have failed to materialize. Isolated fire bombings in Westchester and Bergen counties have produced minor damage, but no known injuries, and the police and fire departments in these communities are now fully mobilized. Armed citizens have been reported at major intersections outside of New York City. In two incidents, a total of three men were wounded when firing broke out between groups of suburbanites believing they had sighted rioters. Harlem itself remains quiet, despite an attack on an elderly black man by a group of young whites who were subdued by local citizens and then arrested. Praise has come in from all sides for the mayor's rapid and effective handling of a dangerous as well as tragic situation. More news in one minute. . . ."

Goldenson switched the radio off and turned to Wendy. "Are you sure you want to stay? It sounds too quiet."

She smiled. "You'd send me home at this late hour?"

"I'd take you home. I'm getting worried. Maybe they're bullshitting about what's happening." His tone was different from before, and he would have been unable to say whether it was the radio broadcast or his time at the enclosure that made the difference.

"It's all right for a man?" She was annoyed.

"It's all right for me because it's my experiment."

"Don't be ridiculous." She wanted to tell him that she cared about him, but something stopped her.

"What do you suggest?" he asked.

"I suggest I stay, just as we planned, and then in the morning, when Hall comes back, if it still looks bad, I'll go, we'll both go."

"And if he doesn't come back?"

She shrugged. It was the closest she could come, right then, to telling him the way she felt. "I'll take my chances."

So Wendy and Goldenson spent the night together in his laboratory. They turned the music on and drank more wine and then made love. And it was freer and more joyous than it had ever been for either of them before. The only explanation was that the danger had set off something new between them.

·7·

EVERYTHING CHANGED the next morning. It happened on East Sixty-fifth Street, at a private rooftop swimming pool, where no black body had ever touched the water, not even to keep it clean. When the pool opened at seven, the usual small group of early risers, executives and professional men, began to arrive. Some may have been early, an indirect result of the panic that was in the air. Perhaps anxiety had awakened them sooner than usual. Others were delayed. Perhaps the *Times* had been insufficient. It may have been necessary to listen to the radio and turn on the television as well. Everyone needed the most current information before stepping outside, even for something as necessary—as life sustaining—as a morning swim. There was still the possibility that the blacks might be up to something, even in that neighborhood, where under normal circumstances a black face out of uniform would be eyed suspiciously by the doormen. But things were under control, the situation quiet, the police still in command, and the usual complement of swimmers did eventually arrive. By seven-thirty that morning there were twelve men paddling slowly, with varying degrees of competence, around the small pool. The warm rays of the morning sun just cleared the edge of the fence and touched the immaculate blue water. A bald man with an enormous paunch, who had been swimming slowly for ten minutes, rested in the warm light and sipped from a coffee cup an attendant placed on the ledge beside him. Another heavy man approached. He was performing an awkward breast-stroke, his body floating high in the water, his buoyancy the only blessing of his thick fat. He winked at the coffee drinker as he went by, but maintained his stroke. A third man, also obese, was holding on to the side of the pool and kicking rhythmically. A fourth man, well built but with a pale lifeless color to his skin and flabby muscles, was floating quietly in the center of the pool while a fifth, at the far end, dove repeatedly from a low board in an awkward imitation of a jackknife.

Not one of the men around and in this pool appeared to be in satisfactory physical condition. They were all between forty and sixty, and all were in some fashion crippled. They were the tennis dropouts, the men too poorly coordinated to play at all or those who once had played but had been warned off by their cardiologists. These men were too decrepit even for jogging, though some did jog occasionally, or had jogged and been told to give it up. They were living testimony to the destructiveness of their high-pressure lives.

"They ought to go in and wipe them out," said the fat man with the coffee cup. "The black ones and the white ones and the brown ones." He was talking to everyone, even those men with their heads in the water, and he was obviously accustomed to being heard. "We've taken enough of their crap. They ruined the city long ago. We ought to put letter bombs in the welfare envelopes." Another man, distinguished looking, slightly British, with gray hair on his head and thick black hair on his chest swam up to him. "We ought to put a wall around the place and blast them into dust. I predict that within five years, if we don't, there won't be anything left of New York."

"I thought it was calm," said the distinguished-looking man.

"What difference does it make? We'd be better off if it wasn't calm. We're only giving them time to make more babies." He placed his coffee cup on the ledge and swam slowly toward the ladder. He pulled himself out quickly and the water poured off of his back in silver sheets. Despite the flab he was clearly still quite powerful. He took a towel from the stack and wiped his face. "Too damn much chlorine," he said, to no one in particular. He wrapped the towel around his shoulders and seated himself so that the sun was on his face. "Tell the lifeguard," he said, assuming that whenever he spoke there would be someone to hear. "And I want another coffee."

The others continued to swim. No one watched the first man leave his chair for a second towel, no one heard him complain that he had a chill. But soon, as others began to leave the water, they could see there was something wrong. He was very pale, and complaining now of nausea. While two others rubbed their eyes and talked about the chlorine he retched his coffee onto the floor. One of the swimmers, a physician, placed his head against the fat man's chest. It didn't sound like a heart attack, but the more he listened the more irregular the beat became. The breathing became more rapid. The man made retching movements, though there was nothing left inside of him, and the physician told an attendant to call an ambulance. Before it arrived the fat man went into convulsions. They tried to make him comfortable. Soon three others, including the physician, were retching, and everyone who had been in the pool was chilled and terrified. It was clear there was something in the water. The police were called, and finally the ambulance arrived. They sent for a second and a third. The swimmers, still in their bathing suits, two of them in comas now, were divided into groups and rapidly taken to the two hospitals in the area.

It was no use. Within two hours eleven of them were dead, and the twelfth, who had been in the water for less than five minutes, was delirious and on the verge of death. There was a chance he would recover, but his brain was certain to be severely damaged. The water of the pool was tested and found to contain a massive quantity of parathion. Someone had dumped several gallons of concentrated poison into the pool and the swimmers had absorbed it through their mouths and eyes and skin.

· 8 ·

GOLDENSON WAS RESTLESS in the night. They slept together in the narrow bed, their bodies wrapped around each other, inside each other. It should have been idyllic. It would have been, except that he cried in his sleep. She clung to him more tightly, pulled his head against her breast, but it didn't help. He struggled hard against her arms. She tried to contain him, soothe him somehow, but the more tightly she held him the more he struggled. Finally she saw that it wasn't helping. That realization was more painful than she would have expected. She let him go, then slowly pulled her arm out from beneath his chest. He seemed to relax a little. She left the bed and crossed the room to examine the clock. It was almost morning anyway; outside the sun would be beginning to rise. Here there was nothing, no trace of the movement of time, only the yellow light of a small lamp on the far side of the room. She had an unbearable sense of his pain. Living in that world, subjecting himself to that schedule; it was bound to make a mess of anyone. She went back to the bed and watched him sleeping there. He was quiet now, a little more relaxed. His body was pale, strong but almost ghostly; it needed the sun, it needed hard physical work, not the unnatural immobility he imposed on it. No wonder he was so tense. She moved closer to his face. He was breathing evenly now, his brown hair on the pillow like a dark star behind him. On his face there was still a frown. He looked worried, his brows compressed as if he was deep in

36

thought. She kneeled beside the bed, overcome by the intensity of her feeling for him, the feeling they found so difficult to talk about. She touched his forehead with her palm and he screamed out loud.

She stepped back. His eyes opened. He looked confused, not yet awake. She came close again and spoke: "It's only me."

"I know," he whispered. "Did I scare you?"

"Did I scare you?" she asked.

"Not you. The dream. It's coming every night."

"Do you want to talk about it?"

"There's nothing to say. There's nothing to it really. Just people all around me, all over me." He looked across the room. "Not even rats, you'd think it would be rats. Just people, people I don't want to see."

She got into the bed beside him and held him in her arms. Now her touch was welcome: more than welcome—necessary. She could feel the tension flow from him. Soon it was replaced by another tension, the one she had been hoping for. They began to kiss and touch each other, and then made love again.

Afterward they slept and he was calm. They awakened late, and she made breakfast. As they ate they listened to the radio. It was hard to know whether to smile or feel sad, and they found themselves feeling a bit of each. The threat of riot was over. There was just some lunatic to worry about. After the danger that had confronted them, he seemed so far away. Wendy bit into a roll. "Just what is parathion anyway?" she asked.

"You never read *Silent Spring*?"

She looked puzzled. "I did read it, yes . . .

"Well then you just forgot the chemicals. Parathion is an insecticide. It doesn't persist in the environment like DDT, it decomposes in a couple of weeks, but it's a lot more deadly. I think a few drops on the skin is enough to put you out. A one way trip." He paused. "Do you want the details?"

She nodded.

"Chemically, it's an organic phosphate, quite different from DDT, which is a chlorinated hydrocarbon. The beauty of parathion is that it acts specifically on the nervous system, either man or bug. The stuff is very similar to nerve gas, and like nerve gas, it was invented by the Nazis," he went on. "Do you want to know how it works?"

She nodded again.

"It interferes with the transmission of nerve impulses," he said. "It destroys the chemical that controls the impulse. Instead of stopping after a particular act, the impulses just go on repeating themselves. They don't get inhibited the way they're supposed to. Like a person would start a lot of things, but he wouldn't get anything done. He would breathe in, and he would keep on breathing in, and he would breathe out, and he would keep on breathing out, and he would do it all simultaneously, along with a hundred other things, because the mechanism that stops all that would have been destroyed."

He looked at her to be sure she followed and then went on: "I can make it more precise. The transfer of an impulse from one neuron to another is helped along by a substance called acetylcholine. It's very tricky, very ephemeral stuff that gets destroyed as soon as a nerve impulse has passed. If it didn't get destroyed, the neuron would go on firing and produce the repetitive state of affairs I just described. Well, fortunately for all of us, God put another magic substance inside the neuron just to get rid of acetylcholine. It changes it into something else, but I won't go into that. You have to realize that I know next to nothing about neurophysiology. I'm just a behavioral psychologist. I don't tinker inside the old black box."

"Just tell me what you know."

"The stuff that destroys acetylcholine is known as cholinesterase, and parathion destroys cholinesterase. It's as simple as that. Parathion destroys cholinesterase."

He looked into her eyes. "Everyone needs cholinesterase. When you run out of it you turn into a twitching, vomiting, convulsing corpse. Your neurons go wild, out of control, and if the dose is strong enough, in a very few seconds you're as dead as those poor bastards in the pool out there. And if it doesn't get you right away, it can catch up on you. The effect accumulates. You may not show symptoms, but every dose of parathion lowers your level of cholinesterase. When it's low enough, when you've had too many tomatoes, it's as bad as jumping into that pool."

She sat there quietly, thinking seriously about the things he had said. "That's what they dump in the ocean?" she asked finally.

"Stronger things, but essentially the same."

"That's what they ship around the country?"

"You get the idea."

"The next time it happens, we protest—"

"I have a better idea," he said.

"Yes?"

"We go away. We leave the scene of the crime."

She shook her head. She didn't believe he was really serious. "I've got too much to do. So do you. Do you mean to tell me you'd give up on your experiment?"

"I think about it every once in a while," he said. Then he looked up at the clock and saw that it was time to go back to work.

·9·

WENDY AND GOLDENSON REMAINED in the lab and worked beside each other. Though the danger outside had eased, they saw no point in taking chances. It would be some time before they could feel safe in Harlem again. In the afternoon there was a thump on the door. They glanced at each other in a brief moment of fear.

"Hey, it's me, said a voice.

They pushed the file cabinet out of the way—they had moved it there the night before—and unbolted the heavy door. It was Ed Hall, looking as if he had not yet slept. "Well . . . the lovebirds," he said, "together in their nest as the whole damn city dissolves into the ground."

"Has it been that bad?" Wendy went for the coffee pot, but he opened the refrigerator and found a can of beer.

"It depends on your point of view. The college has another life. What's the point of burning something that someday you're going to own?" He drank some beer and made an expression of disgust. "The truth is it didn't convince them. They don't believe they'll ever own it, or even attend it, so they won't leave it alone. Nothing of value to black people can ever go on in here. That's their position, to the extent that one could say that they have something resembling a position, a thought-out point of view. What they really have is anger and impulsiveness." He finished the beer and now motioned to Wendy that now he wanted coffee. "I couldn't talk them out of it. I gave up.

I kept my mouth shut." He looked at her. "I would have tried to help you if I got the chance, but I hardly expected to get the chance. I didn't think anything could save the place. Or you. You can thank those twelve white stiffs on the East Side." He looked at Goldenson. "I need some time. One night's sleep. Do you think you can hold the fort until tomorrow. I could be back on schedule by then."

"I don't imagine I have much choice."

Hall's involvement in Goldenson's experiment had begun as an undergraduate honors project. After they became friends, and after Goldenson's grant came through, Hall was awarded a stipend. Though in recent months he had lost some interest in experimental work, had taken to trying to educate a street gang called the Black Angels, he maintained his own shift in the observation schedule and his own share of the data analysis. The publications he was likely to acquire would help his chance for medical school, though it was unlikely, given his straight A average, that he would need much help. "How are the little white buggers getting along?" he asked. "Were they more nervous today?"

"Why don't we have a look?" said Goldenson. "I told you things were happening." At specific periods the schedule re quired them to look for and count specific kinds of behavior. But now they could just relax and wait for something interesting to emerge. It was much more enjoyable than the focused observation, which was only included because two members of Goldenson's thesis committee insisted on it. The three of them went across the room and stationed themselves at separate windows. They could all see into the central area of the enclosure, where the food and water was and where, the night before, Goldenson had observed the litter being born. There was no trace of the mother and her babies now. Large numbers of rats moved chaotically around the feeding area. A tremendous range of activities, from social sniffing of each other to copulation, could be observed. The backs of many of the rats had been stained with different colors: Blue, red, green, yellow, signifying the approximate date of the animal's birth, and there were many smaller unmarked rats that were due to be marked and counted soon.

"Have you had your fill of horror stories?" Goldenson asked Wendy.

"Why do you ask?"

"I could tell you another one."

"If you feel like talking," she said, "go on."

"You know that we're extending Calhoun's work," he said. "We've changed the conditions some, but our results are essentially the same. I told you about the changes in maternal behavior, but that's only a small part of it. We're also observing a pattern called tail biting. I want you to watch, near the water tray, the interactions among those animals."

She saw six rats clustered together in a small group. As another rat approached the water she saw one leave the group and stalk the stranger. Then, quite slowly and deliberately, it bit the other animal at the place where its tail joined its spine. The stranger made no response. It turned its bloody tail away and backed up slowly to the water hole, where it drank rapidly, with its eyes fixed on its attacker. When it finished it backed away, as the attacker returned to its original group. One might have had the fantasy that it was bragging to the others.

"If you followed the aggressive animal you would find that it engaged in such acts an average of once an hour. If you followed the victim, you would find that other rats also attacked it—I can't give you the frequency yet—and that it never took the initiative against some other animal. I don't have all the data yet, but it's a fairly safe prediction that in a week the victim will be dead. The injuries mount up. And tail biting is something that never happens in a normal environment. They don't get close enough. But when the population reaches the right density, a critical mass, it happens all the time. They all get a little kinky. Everyone gets into the S and M trip."

"It's the world of the street corner," said Hall. "I see it all the time."

They continued to watch the animals. "Keep your eyes on the corner opposite the food tray," said Goldenson. A tiny pink creature wriggled blindly across the floor. It was obviously a newborn rat. "Possibly a survivor from yesterday," he said, "though most likely it's from another litter. No matter where it comes from, it has no chance." They watched the tiny creature wriggle aimlessly. It made searching movements with its head for a nipple that would never appear. Its eyes were closed and there was no fur on its body. It was an amorphous, undifferentiated lump—but alive, a complete organism, with the potential to become like the others, perhaps even more than the others. An adult rat approached the baby and sniffed it cautiously. It wriggled with greater intensity, sensing something, but the adult moved away.

"If its mother was around, if it was in anything resembling a nest, that animal would never have approached," said Goldenson. But now the little bugger is fair game. He's gonna end up as someone's dinner. The amazing thing is that, at least for a while, the rats have very strong inhibitions against cannibalism. If it was dead they would eat it, but they'd be reluctant to kill it. Sooner or later a few get the idea, or acquire the habit, however you want to put it. They discover that little creatures taste pretty good. After all, their nutritional value is about the best. So some begin to go after pups. They become the local population controllers. I think you can tell the cannibals just from their physical appearance—they seem larger, their fur has a bit more gloss. You notice that rats under these conditions, even though they have a nutritionally adequate diet, tend to be on the runty side. Well the cannibals hit the high end of the scale."

As he talked they watched a large male rat, one of the group he had just described, edge its way up to the struggling baby. It paused beside it for several seconds. When no angry mother appeared it bit into the pup's neck with what was obviously an accomplished movement. The pup stopped moving and the large rat carried it off to begin its meal.

"Let's take a break," said Wendy. "I think I've seen enough."

"You don't want to work with us?" asked Ed. "You don't want to learn about the future?"

"Not for the time being. I'll stick to ancient history."

Goldenson put his arm around her. "Now you know why I need music. It loosens up my head. It helps connect me with the little creatures. It allows me a little bit, just the tiniest bit, to get inside them."

"Which, of course, is pure fantasy," Ed Hall said.

"Okay, go ahead, my clear-headed colleague, my future

shrink and confidant, why don't you finish the lecture for Wendy. You can brief us on the political and psychological significance of the research."

"I don't make speeches about politics and rats. I learned my science better than that. You taught me better than that. All I will say is that we are at an early stage in an investigation of the effects of an overcrowded environment on the behavior of the albino rat. I could talk about the fact that the rats are albino, but I'll skip that too. The experiment has reached the point that Calhoun called the 'behavioral sink.' There has been a deterioration of the social controls that are characteristic of the animals in a more normal environment. Calhoun demonstrated this, and we've confirmed his results. The question now is what new beast is being born? That's what we want to find out. The question is whether, under more extreme conditions, something new will emerge. Will a new type of social organization come into being? Will new mating patterns, new ways of rearing their young be forced on them? Obviously, when you work with rats the possibilities are limited, but the question is whether even the beginnings of change will occur."

"Like with humans," Wendy said. "Will marriage disappear? Will the commune replace it? Will we have single-parent families?"

"I doubt all of that," he said, "but anyway, you're being too concrete. You can't make the jump from rats to people quite so easily. Believe it or not, we're interested in rats. We're not at all sure that the same thing would be true of people. It might be, but we don't know. It probably wouldn't be the same. Rats don't learn the same way people do, and they don't have a social system. All we can do now is work with our animals. It's much too early to extrapolate."

"Very good," said Goldenson. "Next time you can say it to my class."

"You pay me your salary," said Hall, "and I'll be happy to."

·10·

THE IMAGE ON THE SCREEN was dark and out of focus. At first glance one could hardly make it out: a writhing tangle of body parts—arms, thighs, breasts, buttocks. Only after one looked long and hard enough did it become sufficiently clear. A couple making love—or making something, anyway. Every eye in the theater was glued to the screen, every mouth was slightly open, and almost every lap—at least those in which it was still possible—contained an erection. Something like seventy men were sitting there, at noon on a Monday morning, with the heat and smog unbearable outside, in the cool comfort of the ancient movie house. The air conditioner was on full force, as if in the hope of controlling, somehow, the effect of what was on the screen. But if that was the intention, it had failed. Several men in the audience were masturbating openly, even more were at it beneath their jackets, and no one paid them any mind.

Now the couple shifted position. The woman was atop the man. Her large breasts bounced provocatively as she moved in time with him. Her head was tilted back, her mouth slightly open, and her eyes appeared to be filled with tears. She rocked back and forth, apparently approaching a climax. The music in the background began to build. The camera zoomed in on her breasts; they were covered with an oily sweat.

Suddenly, in the audience, a man screamed. Despite the attraction of the scene in front of them everyone turned to look in his direction. He screamed again, uncontrollably, and rose

45

halfway out of his seat. If it was an orgasm, it was like nothing anyone there had ever experienced, and they all watched intently, not sure for a moment whether to pity or envy him. He screamed a third time and his arms jerked into the air. Then, as abruptly as it came over him, the energy drained away. He slumped across the seat in front of him. The position was unnatural.

The image on the screen blacked out. The lights in the theater came on. The men all looked at each other, frightened at what had happened, uncomfortable with the fact that they could so easily be seen. Several started for the exits. The manager and usher came down the aisle to the man who had collapsed. They lifted him carefully and stretched his body out on the floor. He was a strong looking man, with what at first seemed a ruddy complexion. But as they looked on he grew more pale. The manager lifted the man's hand and tried to feel his pulse. After several attempts he gave it up, and with a grimace of disgust he placed his ear on the man's chest. In a little while he got to his feet and shook his head from side to side. Then he walked slowly to the front of the theater. "Someone seems to have taken sick," he said. "An ambulance is coming. We'll have him on his way to the hospital in a very short time. If you'll kindly take your seats again, we'll be resuming the show right after the ambulance arrives. We can move the film a few minutes back, so you won't miss anything." Finished with his announcement, he started to walk back up the aisle. He looked more upset now. His own face was pale, his own gait wobbly. Halfway up the aisle, on the way to the telephone, he stopped and extended his hands straight out from his sides. He was obviously dizzy. He clutched at one of the seats and retched right there, managing at least to keep his vomit on the bare floor beneath the seat and off the carpet. Then he collapsed completely.

The usher started toward him, but he too had difficulty moving. He sprawled face forward in the aisle. Another man started toward them, but went into convulsions before he had moved two feet. Panic struck the theater now, and whoever was able to move rushed toward the emergency doors.

When the ambulance did arrive, and the police soon after, they were told what happened by the men who made it outside.

Everyone inside the building was dead. But even after they died the air conditioner continued its work. Someone had poured a large quantity of parathion into its filter, and now it exhaled its cool but deadly gas into every corner of the room.

·11·

WENDY NEEDED to see her family. It was a week early, but her father was happy to hear from her. She made the long subway trip to the North Bronx, where he still lived with two of her three younger brothers, and she walked quickly through the familiar, quiet streets, past the cheap but carefully maintained small homes with their asphalt shingles and aluminum siding and lawn animals in their tiny yards. Ever since she left her father's house, at least after the worst of his initial anger, she returned for dinner once a month, and though she knew he was uncomfortable with her feelings and beliefs, the atmosphere between them was affectionate again. Politically and philosophically they were at opposite poles. They disagreed on almost everything. What made it possible for them to talk were the memories that still remained of the time they had lived together and loved each other as a family. Everything was in a kind of balance. They could show certain sides of themselves, discuss certain issues, but never really examine others. Since her mother died while giving birth to James when Wendy was nine, Wendy had been the woman of the house and she had lived that role so fully that it never occurred to her once in the next seven years that any other was remotely possible. Only at the end of her junior year in high school, a Catholic school for girls, did she make the startling discovery that her mind was much quicker than that of most other people, including her teachers. And only after she began to read—not what they gave her in school but things she found on her own in bookstores she discovered on trips out of the neighborhood—did she realize that the world contained alternatives. And in a few years, after she won her scholarship—and not to a Catholic college, where she could never have survived—she simply left the house and went to live in a commune. And though her father cried—literally cried in front of her—and her brothers pleaded and threatened, she stuck to her plan, to the life she had chosen, though she soon enough left that scene and moved into a place of her own.

Her father kissed her now as she entered the house. He looked her over carefully, and if not overjoyed, he was at least not embarrassed. She was wearing her bra. She had passed, long ago, the stage of dressing for the sake of offending him. Now she was more cautious; she was happy to avoid the small battles in the hope that they could pass over the large.

"You look worried," she said to him, "and worn out."

"Everybody's worried," he said. "Aren't you? We're all going nuts, if you want to know the truth."

"I want to hear about it," she said. "It's part of why I came. Everyone I know has got the shakes."

"Just as long as that's all they have, no other symptoms," he said. He looked into her eyes. "I have the shakes myself. If I thought you might listen to me I'd tell you to leave the city. Take a long vacation. Go to the Islands. Hitchhike. Go to a commune." He laughed. "We're no closer to this thing now than we were the first day." He was a lieutenant in the New York City Police Department, had been on the force for more than thirty years. "They're in a panic over this one," he said. "The potential is staggering. The bastards could kill us all, or have us kill each other. Charlie Manson was a piker compared to these sons of bitches."

James, seventeen now, came out of the kitchen with a bottle of whiskey and some glasses. He kissed Wendy self-consciously, then poured a drink for her, as they all took seats in the living room.

"How are things?" she asked James.

"Okay."

"Have you made the big decision?"

"I still have time," he said, looking down at the floor.

"You mean you're having second thoughts?"

Her father swallowed his whiskey and looked at her. "I don't want you to work on him."

"Why not, you and Francis have been doing it all month."

Lieutenant McGhie peered at James, and then back at Wendy. "He knows the alternatives. He's been considering them. You made your case the last time. Now give the boy a chance to make his mind up on his own."

"All I want to say is that if he goes to college he might as well learn something he doesn't already know. There's more to the world than what the Jesuits teach."

"A lot of good it does for you," her father said. They both wanted to stop, and both were unable to.

Her face flushed. She knew that he had once hoped she might become a nun. Now his hopes rested on James. "I'm better off the way I am, better off knowing at least some of the realities of the world and maybe trying to do something about them—"

"Nonsense," her father said. "Don't you think they know about those problems? Don't you think they have any concern?"

"They have concern," she admitted. "It doesn't happen to be enough. What's the point of being concerned about the victims of overpopulation when you're against changing the conditions that produce the victims? What's the point of protecting the fetus if you won't give it a world in which it has some room to grow? I don't see the point in going to a school that builds its whole curriculum around sectarian religious ideas." She was responding to her father, but watching her brother as she talked, trying to tread a delicate path. "I've seen my share of Catholic intellectuals, the few that still believe. They're trapped, they're poor damned creatures, and sexually most of them are a mess."

She had resolved to steer clear of the sexual issue, in any of its forms, at whatever the cost, but here she was bringing it up on her own. She should have stayed away from the population thing too. Her stomach was empty, and she assumed it was the drink, but she lifted her glass anyway and motioned her brother for a refill.

Lieutenant McGhie sat there silently, his own empty glass in his hand. Controlling his last son's education had become increasingly important to him. He was furious at Wendy's attempt to interfere and he thought of telling her to leave. But she was his own daughter and she had been, in her younger days, the best possible help to him, a lifesaver. He could understand her need for liberation; she needed it desperately when she was a kid. Had he known it then he would have done things differently, maybe remarried, maybe hired a maid. But it was too late for that, and he would have to live with her anger and her rebellion as the punishment for what he'd failed to see. He would just have to be patient and accept her, whatever she said or did, whatever sin she committed. Perhaps someday she would come around.

Francis came home now, the oldest son and the one who had followed most closely in his father's footsteps. He nodded at Wendy from the foyer, then stepped into the kitchen for his can of beer, which he carried with him to his room where he removed his gun and uniform. When he returned, in a T-shirt, still in his patrolman's pants, he had, at least to Wendy, the frail and weakened look of someone who has been stripped of the thing most deeply significant about himself. In fact he was anything but frail; he was six feet three inches tall, with broad shoulders, and he had already sprouted a substantial paunch.

Wendy left her seat and patted her brother's tummy. He tolerated her gesture with obvious distaste. "You're coming along nicely," she said. "Are you hoping for a boy or a girl or a hippopotamus?"

"I'm not in the mood for wisecracks," he told her. "I've had a rotten day." The relationship between them had always been quite cool. In recent years it had turned bitter.

"Have they turned up anything new, Francis?" his father asked.

"Not a blessed, bloody thing. They're sitting and waiting and crapping in their pants."

"Watch your mouth," the older man said.

Francis looked at Wendy. "She's liberated, she can listen to it."

"Well, she doesn't have to here."

"It's all right, dad, I don't need protection." She almost called her brother a pig. The word would have upset her father, though she would never have meant it for him. Her father was decent, she knew, willing to follow a kind of code, not a sadist or a sneak like Francis. That feeling dated from the late sixties, when her brother was a part-time informer at the community college he attended. He had turned twenty kids in to the police, mostly for possession of marijuana.

Francis grinned at Wendy. "Let her get protection from her damned hippie lover."

McGhie took him by the arm. "I won't put up with that."

"Okay dad, sorry." The way he looked at Wendy made it clear he was just appeasing his father.

They sat down to dinner. It had been prepared the night before by her father and placed in the oven that afternoon by James. The men bowed their heads as her father prayed for the son who wasn't there: Joseph, the middle boy, an MIA in Vietnam, presumed long-dead. The topic of the war, certain to produce a major fight, absolutely guaranteed to wreck what was left of the evening, was scrupulously avoided by everyone.

"How are your lesbian friends?" Francis asked, still baiting her.

Wendy kept silent, just eating her meal. She knew he was trying to suck her in. He would do anything to make things worse between herself and the others. She also knew that the more aggressive he became, the more provocative, the more obscene, the more James and her father would come to her point of view. She was willing to take his abuse for the sake of that. They weren't fools, they could see right through him. At any rate, it wasn't what he said that bothered her, but the possibility that through his work he had a way of keeping tabs on her. Did he really know anything about her past lovers? About Goldenson? Did he know anything—besides what she had chosen to reveal—about her life? Could he have found out about her abortion? Was it possible that her phone was bugged? Even her apartment? But if he did know anything he would already have told their father. "Could we talk about the killings?" she finally asked. "I'd like to know what's happening."

"Yeah, we could talk about it," said Francis, "but we don't really know that much. Why don't you talk to your hippie friends and find out their latest game. Check it out with the Weathermen. See what Patty's old buddies have to say."

She looked at her brother in disbelief. "You don't know what's happening anymore."

"I know what's happening with you."

Which made her wonder again about how much he did know.

Now it was James who spoke. "Ever since the SLA they've been blaming some kind of radical for every killing they can't solve. It's very convenient."

She felt pleased at James' remark, but tried not to show it. "Really," she asked her father, "is that where they're at?"

He shook his head. "That's just the men in the locker rooms. Sometimes they're more mixed up than the people in the street."

Francis looked at his father. "Then what is going on? Why don't you tell us?"

They all turned to him.

"Between us at this table?" McGhie asked. "To stay within these walls?"

They all nodded. It was the moment—the same as years ago—when he used to tell them something special about a case, something that would put them a few days ahead of the newspapers. They were a family again, united in their expectation.

"Nothing."

A tremendous letdown. Also terrifying.

"Nothing at *all?*" she asked.

He sipped a glass of beer. "There are some leads," he said. "Possibilities. Hundreds of them. Who could have known about this poison? Where could he have gotten it? Why would he have wanted to? What links up the groups of people murdered? Like I've told all of you a thousand times, police work isn't dramatic. You have to plod along. It takes a good accountant. In a couple of years it'll all be done by computers. Right now it still takes a lot of time. It takes patience. By tomorrow morning we expect a report from a laboratory comparing the three different samples of the poison. Did it all come from the same place? Can we determine the place he got it? Why haven't they reported it missing? If we can answer that one we'll at least have made a dent." He looked more and more upset as he went on. "The trouble is, it takes time. Much too much time. He could kill us all before we got even warm. The mayor likes to pretend we're close. He has to do it, to calm things down, make people less afraid, keep them from killing each other again. The fact is we're *not* close. We're not close at all." He shook his head from side to side. It was becoming clear to Wendy how profoundly upset he really was. "We're taking precautions about food and public facilities," he went on. "We can make things more difficult for him. But that's what we're reduced to, defensive stuff."

"You're talking as if it's one person," Wendy said. "And certain to be a man."

"We're not even sure of that," he admitted. "It's just an assumption we make in cases like this. It usually is a man. If it's a woman, like that time in California, she's usually ordered to do it by a man. A man did it to those people in the VA hospital. A man shot those people in Ohio. Things like this happen all the time, on a smaller scale, and almost always it's a man."

"But you could be wrong." She felt about ten years old.

"Of course we could be wrong. We go with the probabilities. The computer would tell us to look for a man. Not an organization. Not a group. Not even hippies or revolutionaries. A single man with a heavy grudge. Someone that some psychiatrist will eventually get off the hook."

"And if that doesn't work you pick the next most probable solution." She made an unhappy face.

"What do you expect?" he asked. "What else should we do? Take the least probable?"

"I'm tempted to say yes. Nothing works the way it's supposed to. The laws of probability don't apply. Your laws don't apply." She had started out to make a point but found, halfway into it, that she was no longer clear about what she meant to say. Nevertheless, she was drunk enough to go on with it: "You have to get free of the rigidities. Not trapped by your categories. Free to think of things that won't fit the system. Not pushed in one direction by some narrow computer-type pseudo-logic. Able to use your intuition. This whole stupid crazy situation goes beyond all the old laws. Everything's different now—"

"And we should use a woman's intuition?" Francis asked, with a toothy smile. "That would really solve it, I suppose."

You creep, she said to herself.

Now they ate silently. The food cleared her head, and Wendy wondered what she had been up to. Was it all about her past inside the family? Was it about the way they defined things, their rigidity, their fucking categories? That they thought that being intuitive was being feminine and had to bury that side of themselves or risk thinking that they might be gay? The fact that Goldenson didn't work that way was one of the things that made him special. But was that what bothered her, or was it all the killing? They were sitting there and waiting for another set of murders to change the probabilities. Very slowly, as more people died, as more bits of information came in, they assumed their odds would improve. She could see the point. She could think that way, it was just that they couldn't accept her way at all—her despised unscientific intuition—

"How are the rats?" Francis asked.

The question jarred her back into the room. For a moment it made no sense to her, and she felt defenseless. "They're fine," she replied cautiously.

"People like that have no respect for anything"—she stared as he went on—"they claim to study nature but they mostly want to destroy it. They put innocent animals through every damn kind of torture they can think of. They call themselves scientists, but it's all for the sake of some phony career—"

"What are you *talking* about?"

"Your boyfriend the professor."

"A reverence for life," she said, and shook her head. "You certainly find it in the most unlikely places."

"Well, I do have that," he said. "Not like the creeps you hang around with. I do believe in life. I believe in the right to life. That's more than I can say for the likes of you."

"This is getting boring," she said quietly. She got to her feet and began to carry dishes to the sink.

They all looked at her with surprise; it was the first time she had helped with the dishes in years. "I'll take care of this," she said. "You can sit in the other room."

And at least for a moment she made it seem as it had once been for them so long ago.

·12·

THE CITY RETURNED to a kind of calm. The fact that the latest victims had been watching a pornographic movie made the incident mildly amusing and subtracted significantly from the horror of its reality. Everyone could say that they got what they deserved. God had punished them. And now a week had passed with nothing new. The newspapers were filled with articles about parathion—the problems of detecting it and the details of its cumulative effect. Every prior exposure from agricultural work in a field that had just been sprayed to faint traces on contaminated fruit, lowered a person's tolerance and made it that much more likely that he would die when exposed to the chemical again. And there was no simple way one could be sure of what one's exposure had been, no way to tell how much poison there already was in one's system.

There was a numbness in the air, in part the result of the unbearable heat and the frequent brownouts. A layer of pale gray smog had settled in again, it seemed forever this time. It was always a little hard to breathe, to move around, to be certain that one wasn't already showing signs of something. Beneath the lethargy, beneath the superficial calm, was panic—a sense, perhaps pushed away, of how vulnerable everyone was to the kinds of death that had occurred. On top of everything, because of the power problems, the air conditioning was unreliable.

Early in the summer there had been a major smog alert, a

potential disaster much worse than the murders, threatening the lives of thousands, and the mayor had ordered, routinely, that the burning of refuse be stopped. It had seemed a small gesture, necessary but minor, until the trash began to accumulate so rapidly that no one could think of what to do with it, and it rotted in huge piles along the waterfront and even threatened the city with a possible plague. The idea of burning the garbage had to be considered again, though now the air had grown much worse. Such alternatives as dumping it into the ocean on an outgoing tide were also proposed, but several Long Island beach communities threatened vigilante action if necessary. It still might have been attempted if there'd been the boats to handle it, and if the sanitation men hadn't refused to go near the garbage unless they received an exorbitant rate of pay.

People were forced to become aware, in a way they had never been before, of the interdependence of all their lives. They were forced to begin to see themselves as connected with their environment in an intricate and delicate system, and they couldn't help but feel how vulnerable they all really were. Every part of the system was affected by alterations in every other part, including parts over which they had not one bit of control. There was always the possibility that some obscure person with some obscure responsibility would do something or not do something that no one else would know or think about until the city came crashing down. And the more aware they became of this fact of their existence, the more depressed they all became. It was The Bomb again, but in another form. The more they tried to think about it, the more complex they saw it to be, the more out of control they saw it was, the closer they came to feeling that everything might be hopeless. . . . Solomon Goldenson had taken that sort of depressing trip long before it lay on the city like the shroud of its dead air. He had been in it and overwhelmed by it and literally immobilized by it.

It had begun while he was in college, fifteen years before, majoring in biology, the subject he'd loved ever since he had been a child. His depression came when he was studying the effect of DDT on birds, the fact that it caused many species to lay eggs without shells, or with shells so thin that they were useless.

It struck him then that maybe there was just no point in learning biology. It also struck him that there was maybe no point in learning anything . . . it was all over, life on earth was finished, it was already too late. . . . And though he had known that his conclusion was premature, based perhaps on something inside himself, the idea had more power in it than any interpretation. And he became an egg born to the eagles—without a shell, with a membrane so thin and fragile that the slightest touch would penetrate. It was much more than a touch that he'd already felt.

That was when he'd left school. The years between that first experience of near hopelessness and the place where he was now were little more than just a blur. A necessary blur. He had distorted the world or blocked it out in order to protect his fragile self. To live without a shell was as impossible for him as for the birds. He tried to grow a shell that he could respect. That period had lasted for ten years—through Europe and India and Mexico and the Rocky Mountains. He came back to a vision of life and his own place in it that once had seemed impossible. Not perfect. Maybe not forever, but with a place in it where he could live and work. He turned back to the belief that it did make sense to try to understand. If one were careful, and asked the right questions, it might be possible to understand. Not through mysticism. Not through drugs. But through study, observation, science. Everything might come together, he might even have some effect on something.

And he developed hope again. A kind of shell. Permeable to some things, impermeable to all the rest, himself choosing. The hope of change. Of being reasonable, clear. Of understanding nature. The hope of finding a solution, of making a contribution, of stopping the process that seemed so certain to destroy. It was a way of atoning for something destructive he sensed inside himself, a way of attempting to pay nature back, to redeem a little of the debt he owed the birds. . . .

Now Solomon Goldenson was seated at his window, where he'd been in carefully measured intervals for the past six hours. He turned the music up, a Beethoven symphony, but he still found it hard to keep his eyes wide open. His lids kept closing halfway and his head kept nodding forward only to snap up suddenly as he caught some fragment of something interesting.

In part he was seeing the animals, in part he was watching his dream. The rats were behaving predictably. They had paused in their growth toward whatever was to come. Nothing happened smoothly, but in fits and starts and awkward jumps. Wendy would know about it; she'd tell him the latest historical theory. Then his head drooped forward again. He was too tired to go on. He had lost track of what he was looking at. He was about to stop when his attention was caught by one of the larger rats and his drowsiness suddenly disappeared.

The animal slowly circled the enclosure, avoiding contact with any of the others, a noteworthy fact in an environment where social interplay was constant. It watched the feeding tray in the center of the enclosure, where dozens of rats were clustered, as if it was seeking something. For at least five minutes it just kept circling slowly.

Goldenson had no idea if the rat had a specific purpose. All he could see was that its concentration was unique and that, among the stunted creatures in the enclosure, it looked quite large, well fed. He assumed from that that it was a cannibal, perhaps one of the type Calhoun described, an abnormal group he had labeled "probers."

Now the rat edged closer to the central group. It seemed almost nonchalant. Perhaps it was just going to join the others. With a lightning move, equally surprising to Goldenson and to the victim—and almost equally painful—it leaped on the back of another rat. The victim was immobilized as the aggressor made rapid-thrusting sexual movements. In seconds it leaped away, leaving the victim bleeding from a bite on its neck and from beneath its tail. In his dreamy state Goldenson lost distance between himself and the animals. It felt like he had been raped himself. There was a rush of anger. He wanted to go into the enclosure and punish the rat. He would wring its neck or drop it into the jar of chloroform. He restrained himself. There was nothing for him to do but watch. That was all he ever had to do. He turned away from the bloody victim and scanned the enclosure for the attacker. It was gone. There were just too many animals. It had a blue stain on its back, but that wasn't enough to identify it. He would just have to wait until it struck again and he was there to see it. He turned back to the victim, a scrawny young creature with a green mark on its back, part of the generation just coming into maturity. Now she had another, growing, stain from the wound on her neck. He wondered if there was something special about her that stimulated the attack? Had she provoked it? The possibility that he had seen something important occurred to him. Perhaps her body chemistry had changed; maybe she smelled different to the other animals. Calhoun found changes in liver functioning and vitamin E metabolism in his experiments. But if she had changed physiologically it would have to be something specifically sexual. Perhaps she was in heat, but in an abnormal way. A change like that could disorient a male. It would be important to autopsy her, examine her endocrine system, find out what the factor was, or at least make a stab at it.

Goldenson removed his earphones. He had to go into the enclosure and remove the dying animal. He studied her carefully to make certain he would not confuse her with another. Then he went to the small door at the edge of the structure. Holding his breath, he stepped in. He was enveloped at once by the heavy animal warmth of the place. The ventilating system never quite got rid of that. Rats so close to each other generated considerable heat. It felt the way the subway did after a long hot week. The animals began to squeal and crowd each other in their rush to avoid him. They pressed into the far corner of the enclosure, where some were certain to be crushed. It happened every time. They never developed the trust of humans that laboratory animals usually acquired. With his breath still held, as if something within that place might slip inside him if he inhaled, he reached for the dying rat. It made a feeble effort to wriggle away, but he netted it easily. Now he backed out the door and closed it carefully. He took a deep breath as he carried the animal across the room. He removed the cover of a large glass jar. On the bottom it held a sponge that had been soaked in chloroform. The rat was too weak to struggle much as he dropped it in and screwed the lid on tight. He left it alone to inhale the lethal fumes, not pausing to watch it as it died.

Goldenson returned to the enclosure. He reached automatically for his earphones but the music had already stopped. He remained beside the window. There was something bothering him. He felt he had left something undone or seen something important that failed to register. He was trying again to find the animal that raped the one in the jar. Again he thought that he might punish it. He would put it in a separate cage. He'd imprison it and wait for Wendy to apply the punishment. Rape was now political too. It had to do with power between the sexes. He was falling into the reverie again, and knew he had to pull away.

He returned to the dead rat and removed it from the chloroform. He began to wrap it in a plastic bag. Now he remembered what had been bothering him, and he examined the genitals of the dead animal. It had not been penetrated in the way he thought. He felt a kind of outrage and a twitch of fear. The blood was oozing from its anus; the victim had been a male.

·13·

IN THE MORNING Goldenson felt disgusted with himself. He should never have given up, never have gone to bed without locating the aggressive animal. He had hardly been able to sleep anyway, with images of that strange rat in his dreams and flashes of rage at it filling his night. He made coffee for himself and brought the cup to the window of the enclosure. He had nothing scheduled. The day had been planned as one of rest, an opportunity to relax outside, to get some sun on his pallid skin. Under other circumstances he might have fought the oppressive crowds and taken the subway out to Brooklyn and to the beach where he might join yet another oppressive crowd. But the radio reported an oil slick, and with the killer still on the loose the idea was considerably less tempting than it once might have been. He would spend the day in the lab. It was cool and safe and comfortable. He had to locate the animal. Nothing else really mattered. He thought again of the attack he had seen the night before, and again he felt like a fool. The rat was exactly the kind of creature his experiment was designed to create. What happened was exactly the kind of bizarre behavior he had been looking for. For some dumb reason he let it slip through his fingers. Maybe not so dumb. Maybe there was a meaning to it. Maybe he didn't want to see it. Maybe it was time to quit. That thought hung there. He felt that disgusted. Maybe he had lost interest. Maybe the work was turning into the kind of empty ritual research became for so many others.

Maybe it was time to give up and go away, get on the road again, or into the woods. Maybe he was just afraid.

The possibility of giving it up, more and more attractive, remained in Goldenson's mind. It took as much effort to stop something that was wrong as it did to begin something that was right. But the experiment was right, he had no doubt of that, and no passing setback or temporary terror would change his mind. Even if it never worked out, even if the results failed to follow the direction he anticipated, it would still have been a worthwhile idea. Now he wondered why he was thinking like that. Things *were* going in the way he anticipated. He was on the track of something. Then, abruptly, with no thought leading up to it, just out of the blue, he knew the answer. It was too horrible, just too horrible. It was only a dream he once had, only a fantasy. He never intended to make it real. There had been comfort in the fact that that was what it was, a fantasy, an abstract formulation. It was the way he lived his life. He never meant to prove that it could really happen, never meant to turn his inner world into something real.

Now he sat beside the enclosure, not looking at anything inside, just clinging to the coffee cup. It was like finding out, all at once, that one's worst fears about oneself are true. The world inside the enclosure was only an extension of his inner world. Then he smiled. The thought was overwhelming, and also absurd. In his next life he would go into analysis. There was some comfort in that—it was always a possibility. Then he looked through the window again, alert to what was happening. Maybe the animal wouldn't be so horrible. Maybe it would have some redeeming feature. He sat there, finishing his coffee and then hardly moving, for three hours. He tried to focus and at the same time remain open to something new. He watched the mass of animals on the floor of the enclosure, scurrying in what at first glance always seemed random patterns but then, on closer inspection, always had some specific meaning, some specific goal. They ate and drank, socialized and groomed each other, mated and explored. He scanned the sides of the enclosure, where animals traversed the open shelves and platforms, where some females still managed successfully to rear their young, where something resembling a normal life for the rats was still possible, enclaves controlled by a small number of dominant males who managed to protect their own territory and who could attract and hold a harem. He looked carefully at each of these animals. Like the one he was searching for, they tended to be large. Many of them were marked with blue dye and it was impossible to know if the one he was looking for was among them.

Then he noticed something a little strange. On a high shelf, in a place from which it could observe almost everything, almost out of his field of view, was a solitary rat with a blue mark on its back. It was sleeping there, its head at the edge. He moved to another window, for a better view. The size was right, but the rat was positioned where it could not be clearly seen. For half an hour he sat there as the animal slept. Finally, in irritation, he tapped the window once with the end of his pen. The animal opened its eyes. It gave no indication of surprise. Without moving its head it looked at the place he had struck. He had the feeling it was looking through the silvered glass and into his eyes. For a moment he felt the impulse to turn away.

At last the creature moved. It stretched slowly, still looking in Goldenson's direction. Then it went to the ramp that led down to a lower shelf and from there to a larger ramp that descended to the floor. Its movements were slow and seemed more cautious than those of the average rat, and it engaged in no social behavior. A feeling of great excitement came over Goldenson. He was into a fantasy again. His initial fear had passed. He had the image of a fat monarch, a king or dictator, descending from the heights to mingle with his subjects without their knowledge. He was filled with a kind of envy. Was it real, or was it his fantasy? The rat appeared at ease, comfortable with itself and its surroundings. Was it a new kind of creature? A mutant? A rat that could master the world in which it found itself, the grotesque world he had dreamed of and then created? He was in awe of its ability to survive, the fantastic ability of life to adapt to new conditions, and yet there was also a hatred of it, for the new habits it had acquired. He knew that this was the animal he had seen last night, the pervert that had raped and killed the other rat. The certainty burned in him. It was a "prober," to use Calhoun's term, but much more than a prober. It was the creature that came after probers, the next adaptation. Goldenson watched the rat amble up to the water tray. The other animals edged slowly away. They knew something. It drank its fill. When a young rat came too close it slashed out and left the little one bleeding. The movement of its hind legs had been as fast as a karate chop, and as devastating; the wounded rat would soon be dead.

Goldenson was now certain that he had seen something of real importance. This rat had an intelligence and a dedication to the death of others he had never heard of before. He could recognize the animal now, could probably pick it out of any dozen, but he needed a way of finding it in the midst of hundreds, of seeing where it was and what it was up to at any time. He would have to mark the rat in some special way, place some color on its fur that would enable him to spot it at a glance. He knew what he had to do, but he was unable to leave his perch beside the window. There was just too much chance that the rat would move and become indistinguishable again. He sat there for another hour as it went slowly about its business, apparently inspecting the cage, never bothering to approach the food hopper but instead killing and eating a newborn pup. It occurred to Goldenson that the fact that it didn't eat beside the others, in the forced sociability of the feeding situation, was perhaps a clue to its deviant development. Then he saw it ascend the ramp. Very slowly, as if it knew it was being observed, with the same regal bearing as before, it returned to its prior perch, placed its head on the edge, and closed its eyes.

When it was asleep for fifteen minutes Goldenson made his move. Very cautiously and slowly he edged away from the window. At the far end of the lab he found the bottle of red dye that he had used to stain the backs of an earlier generation. He put on a pair of heavy cloth gloves and went to the door of the enclosure, where he kept his net. Then he slowly opened the door. His movements were so deliberate that this time he hardly disturbed the animals. When the door was open he stepped inside. There was the same heat, the same animal smell. It felt as if he was standing beside some immense single organism instead of several hundred small ones. He moved very slowly away from the door, closer to the huge creature that was now in his mind, then pulled the door shut behind him. The rats edged away, but showed no sign of their usual panic. He felt now that they accepted him. He was one of them, a part of them. He looked for the rat he was hoping to mark. It hadn't moved. Its eyes were open and it met his gaze. It was going to be tricky. He had to be sure not to injure it. He began, slowly, to raise the net. If he could just flip it over the rat, the rest would be simple. But as he reached the level of its perch the rat began to back away. It moved quite cautiously, watching him all the while, in the direction of a ramp that would take it to another shelf. Goldenson moved more quickly, and the rat increased its speed. He lunged and it leaped away. It reached the ramp and started down. If it made it to the floor, to the other rats, his task would be impossible, he might even lose it. He feinted, trying to cut off its path to the ground. The animal refused to be cowed. It leaped off the ramp. When it hit the floor it would be in the midst of all the others. He stabbed with the net and managed to catch it in the air.

It was a lucky break, but there was no time to savor it—the animal was already scrambling up the mesh and attempting to escape. He lowered the net quickly and flipped it over on the floor. Now the animal was trapped. He crouched on the floor beside it as the other rats scurried away. It squealed once, quite loudly, and then began to tear at the mesh. He placed one hand over the animal's body. He could feel it wriggling powerfully against his grip. Then it twisted its head around and bit into his protective glove. With his free hand he poured the red dye over the rat's back. He covered a large area, much larger than his usual application, and it spread all over his net and gloves and on the floor. When it was done he removed the net. The animal seemed stunned. It was facing away from him, and it failed to move. It shook its body and sprayed red dye around the cage. Then it turned toward him. It was now, truly, a bizarre creature. Its head and neck were crimson, its shoulders and back pale blue, and where the colors overlapped, a deep purple could be seen. It was absurd, clownlike, ridiculous as it stood there looking at him, and he could see, in its eyes, the intensity of its terror, and its rage.

•14•

NEXT THE KILLER got to the water supply. People began to die at home. Some were rushed to the hospital, but they died there as well, less comfortably. It was the familiar set of symptoms. At first it seemed to the victims that they had a simple cold: they would feel the chills, the nausea, the aches and pains, and an overwhelming urge to rest in bed. There they would remain. They might make matters worse by drinking tap water. Depending on past exposure to insecticides—available cholinesterase—and on the amount of parathion in the water, and on the quantity of water they drank, the symptoms might persist for hours, days, or weeks. They might be mild. But eventually the convulsions came, and the coma, and the grotesque death.

As a result of recent experience, the resources of the city were quickly brought to bear. The physicians were able to determine, almost immediately, that the new outbreak was also due to parathion. The police attempted to locate the source geographically. In time-honored fashion they plotted each death on a map of Manhattan. It soon became obvious that they followed a quite specific pattern. There were streets on which large numbers of people were affected and adjacent streets where no one had gotten sick at all. There were streets that reeked with the smell of death and streets that only smelled of smog and garbage. They focused on the fact that no one living north of East 73rd Street was affected. From that point south there was a large concentration of deaths that

67

spread out in all directions but north, and gradually diminished. The center was a point on Madison Avenue, where the first and greatest number of deaths took place. It was if someone had splashed the poison up against a map of the city and allowed the stuff to drip down and out from where it struck. One look at that map by an engineer from the Department of Water Supply established the certainty that one of the large city water mains was the point of entry.

From there on it was legwork: tracking down the false leads and finally zeroing in on the source. They located a basement studio that had been rented by a photographer. He had done some work there, the superintendent said, but never moved much equipment in. In fact he hadn't been seen for over a week. They didn't wait for a key. Inside, the place was bare. He had obviously done no work at all. In a corner, behind a brick pillar, one of them saw a leg. They found him dead beside a faucet. He had just taken a drink, and died right there. They were so close to the source that the concentration was lethal immediately. They sent men out at once to examine the surrounding houses.

In another basement, also recently rented, they found what they were looking for. The killer—and now they were sure it was one man—had dug down into the water main. He even left a map that showed its exact location, less than ten feet below the ground. With the elaborate tools he'd left behind he had broken through cement and stone, then drilled into the water main itself. A pumping device atop the main was attached by hose to a black plastic fifty-gallon drum. With that much parathion he might have killed half the city. It was all so simple. One wondered why it had never happened before. It was recalled in the newspapers that not long ago the CIA had been forced to reveal a set of plans that examined exactly that possibility.

And when the word went out again—people had to be warned about the water—the feeling among the survivors reached new intensities of terror. Thousands left the city, simply packed their bags and went away without a thought of where exactly they were going or how they would survive. They only found that others, outside the city, treated them as if they were the poisoner himself, as if they carried traces of contamination with them. And those who were trapped in the city, who saw no hope of getting out, turned from terror to a kind of mindless rage. There was rage against all institutions of power and the people who worked in them. The mayor received two hundred threatening telephone calls, the police commissioner fifty. Two policemen were killed in what appeared to be random and unrelated attacks: one struck down by a taxicab—witnesses said intentionally—as he directed traffic in front of a Brooklyn school, the other disarmed by a group of youths and thrown from a bridge between Manhattan and the Bronx, in full view of at least one hundred motorists caught in a traffic jam, most of whom cheered as the man was flipped over the rail. The amount of street violence and family violence abruptly skyrocketed.

It was only the fact that, finally, there was the beginning of a real lead that stopped the outbreaks and focused attention back on the killer himself. The landlord who rented the basement survived the poisoning. Though he lived in the building—a fact apparently known to the killer—and almost certainly would have been poisoned, he had left for a vacation in Florida two days before the deaths began. They were able to locate him and obtain their first description of the killer. He was just a "regular looking person," the landlord said. He was a tall, broad-shouldered man, with blue eyes and black hair and some freckles on his face. His hair was short, his appearance neat, his clothing conservative. It wasn't a great deal, but compared to what they had before it was everything. After the landlord sat down with the police artist and the computer, they even came up with a sketch. But the picture was so ordinary looking that they were afraid to risk its distribution for fear it would lead to attacks on innocent persons. As expected, there were no fingerprints. He would have had to be a fool to handle chemicals like that without a pair of gloves, and though many thought him crazy, no one could say he was a fool. So the landlord's description was all they had. The trouble was, it didn't fit what they were hoping for. They had been convinced he would be something different: a freak, a cripple, some kind of mad scientist, someone with some obvious reason to feel such hate. Instead it seemed, from the way he looked, that he was just like anyone else.

·15·

"I NAMED HIM IRVING," Goldenson said. "After my big brother. I always felt he was out to get me."

Wendy, Goldenson, and Hall were seated beside the enclosure waiting for the animal, asleep on its perch, to wake and do something interesting.

"Do rats dream?" she asked.

"They have sleep cycles," said Hall, "and rapid eye movements. When humans have REM and you wake them, they tell you they just had a dream."

"So what would a rat dream about?" she asked.

"Its past, its current life, its future," said Goldenson. "Life in that fucking tank. Why should they be any different from the rest of us?"

"I could give you about a thousand reasons," Hall said quietly.

"He's waking up," Goldenson whispered.

The rat's eyes opened and he stretched. He looked large, but not malevolent, not quite what Goldenson had led them to expect. He was even slightly ridiculous with his red and blue and purple coloring. He circled the platform slowly, as if checking to be certain that his special place was undisturbed. Another animal, also larger than the rats below, with a blue mark on its back, from the same generation, perhaps even the same litter, a brother or sister, came up the ramp. The rat Goldenson had named "Irving" was at the far end of the platform as the other animal came into view. Irving sat up on his hind legs, motionless, in a gesture that seemed just curious. The new rat, unchallenged, slowly approached to sniff its greeting. It seemed a calm, conventional interchange. But a split second before their noses touched, Irving jumped aside, then leaped on top of the visitor from behind and bit its neck. When he got off, the blue mark on the other rat's back was covered with blood. The animal seemed dazed, unable to respond to the attack. It was unequipped for such an assault. There was nothing in its experience or in its genes that might have prepared it. All it could do was circle slowly, in its own weakening confusion, as blood flowed down its neck and formed a puddle at its feet. The animal was dying rapidly as Irving watched from across the platform. After it collapsed, but well before it died, Irving approached again and began to drink the blood.

"Call him Dracula," said Hall.

Goldenson shook his head from side to side. "I can't believe it," he said. "This really is something new." There was a dazed quality to his voice, as if he'd been attacked himself. . . .

Now the rat was dead, and they watched in horror as Irving chewed into its abdomen.

"The liver," Goldenson whispered. "He must need vitamins."

The situation was grotesque, but also remarkable. It was the ability of life—some kind of life, any kind of life—to prevail. There was a fantastic effectiveness to Irving's activities. He seemed to know exactly what his body needed, and how to get it. There was a quality of consciousness he seemed to have, a sense of his environment and his place in it that distinguished him from all the others. Goldenson wondered whether he would be as comfortable in another environment, one more natural, more like the kind in which a normal rat would thrive. Another experiment suggested itself: to place Irving—and other Irvings that might appear—in an environment that wasn't overcrowded. What would happen to him there? Would he be unable to take the solitude? Would he still be dominant? Would he become the weakest? No time to deal with such questions now. The future of Irving was the central issue. Goldenson felt a rush of sadness ... he was caught, they all were, by things they didn't seem able to control. ... What was happening in the city seemed proof of it. All they could do was sit there, and look into the enclosure, and ...

"I've created a monster." He didn't mean it as a joke. "I feel like Dr. Frankenstein. Maybe the kids on campus are right, maybe I should never have started this."

The telephone rang. Wendy answered it. She motioned to Hall.

"Yes," he said into the telephone, then listened. "When?" he asked. "Where is she?" He turned slowly to Wendy and Goldenson, looking dazed, another victim. "My mother's in the hospital. Parathion. I have to go."

When Hall was gone Wendy embraced Goldenson. It wasn't sexual—she realized he felt he was falling apart, that things were closing in ... the world had too often been unbearable for him, and now his experiment had become unbearable as well. It had once been his own world, his own creation, a place for his fantasy, the only thing he completely controlled, a refuge from the world. Controlled horrors. Now it was not so simple. The boundaries were breaking down, the window cracking. Inside and outside were becoming indistinguishable. ...

"Let's get out of here," he said, the strain in his voice quite clear.

"Where to?"

"Out to the country, into the woods, away from this fucking insanity."

She looked him in the face. "A month ago you were ready to stick it out in the middle of a riot." She went to the refrigerator. There was an open bottle of wine and she poured a large glass for him.

"I was a dope," he said. "I thought life was very simple. I was confused. Too much time in the basement—it weakened my brain. Too many fantasies." He took the wine she offered and drank it quickly.

"I don't think this is the time to think about it," she said. "I think you're too upset." She sipped a small amount from her own glass. "I think it's something to hold in the back of our heads. It's a possibility. It always was a possibility for you, but maybe this time it calls out a little more . . ." She was trying to calm him. It didn't matter what she said. There was a look on his face she had never seen before, a look of genuine horror. The juxtaposition of the rat's attack and the news about Hall's mother had devastated him.

"I admire the bastard, and I despise him." He shook his head. "Can you believe I'm talking this way about an animal?"

She waited, and sipped her wine. The best thing would be to get him drunk. "What do you admire and what do you despise?" She sipped from her glass again in the hope that he would imitate her, and he finally did.

"The fact that he can make it. The fact that he can act. I admire that. That he can take things as they come and turn them to his advantage. That he can rise above the others." He drained his glass. "Fuck it," he said. He got to his feet and went back to the window.

"What are you up to now?"

"I can't keep away. I can't look, and I can't keep away."

There was nothing to do but pour more alcohol into him. She went to the refrigerator, opened another bottle and held it in her lap as she sat beside him at the enclosure. She was afraid of what he might do next. She was afraid he might end the experiment. Then she saw that he was calm. It occurred to her that looking again might be a good idea. He would come to terms—or try to come to terms—with whatever was eating at him. He'd never been able to escape it, maybe he could go down into it and through it. It would be another trip; his own lifelong trip, the trip he was taking in his work. . . . The trouble was that it had gone too far; it had become too complex and too inclusive; it threatened to include everything in his life and future. And then she grasped something more of what he was experiencing. It wasn't just the horror—he'd dealt with that before—it was the fact that the horror had gone beyond the experiment. The killer outside and the killer inside had become connected. The thought that they were linked was what disturbed him. He was like the rat, and the rat was like the killer. It gave him another reason to be afraid of what was inside himself. . . .

"He's . . ." Goldenson began a sentence, then paused, obviously feeling the wine. He smiled, partly to Wendy, but mostly, it seemed, to no one in particular. The rat was on the floor of the enclosure in the midst of a group. "He's . . . faking it." He smiled again before going on. "Getting in good with the boys." He giggled aloud and squeezed her shoulder.

"What?" she asked. "What are you talking about?"

He didn't answer, apparently absorbed in watching Irving as he drifted with the group of rats. The colored markings on their backs were all different, indicating that they came from different generations, but there was a preponderance of green indicating a large concentration of young rats, the last group Goldenson had marked. The animals mingled with the others, appeared to engage in a variety of interactions, and then regrouped at the far end of the enclosure.

"I don't . . . believe it," Goldenson said, and she thought as she looked at him that he was shifting back again into his reverie of terror.

"You don't believe what?"

"An army. The marines. The Green Berets, the fucking Green Berets."

As if at a signal, the rats followed Irving up one of the ramps. At first they moved slowly, but as they approached their goal— a shelf on which two females had built their nests—they all were running at top speed. "Mylai," he said. The rats attacked. Irving went for the male that tried to defend his territory. The others slashed at everything available—the females, their young, and at each other. It became a shrieking, savage melee, the sounds audible outside the enclosure. Within thirty seconds every animal on the shelf, with the exception of Irving, had sustained a serious wound. The blood dripped down to the main floor below, where other rats lapped it up, and wounded animals flopped against each other.

Wendy turned to Goldenson, whose face was a mask, as if what he was feeling, thinking, was too awful to show.

"It was all worked out," he said after a long silence. "Down to the smallest detail. No rat ever managed that before. At least none I ever heard of." He shook his head from side to side. "Not a random creation. I don't believe it. Not an accident. Something very specifically related to the life in there. Old patterns adapted to new conditions. A monster emerges. A brilliant monster. More brilliant than the others, though they're all brilliant, any living thing is brilliant, any thing that once was alive—"

"Why does it kill?" she asked.

His voice was a monotone: "A mechanism. An adaptive mechanism no one knows about yet. A reaction to these conditions. Where's the wine?" She poured another glass. "An innate releasing mechanism. Call up Konrad Lorenz, ask for his opinion. You know, some animals, when there are too many, run into the sea. Others migrate. In an aggressive species, why shouldn't one begin to kill. Murder in the service of survival." He drained his glass and went on again in a slightly more expressive voice. "When you come down to it, he's doing good. Making sure that some survive. Making sure they're not wiped out by disease or famine. They may not know how much they need him. They may not appreciate his gifts. Like we approve of his results but deplore his methods . . ." He paused. "One problem . . . only one small cloud . . . he may not stop. I mean it took a lot for him to start, there's no guarantee he'll turn it off . . ."

"You mean when the population goes down enough?"

"Right."

"Then what would happen?"

"How would I know?" He seemed to be feeling again, and with the return of feelings he was becoming more upset. "He'll kill them all. He's making room. He's bringing down the population, but *not for them*. They blew their chance. He's making room for another colony, a different colony." His eyes opened wide as he was struck by another idea. "A cancer," he said. "It's run out of things to eat and so it eats itself."

Later, in the bed beside him, as he tossed and turned and hung on to his pillow, Wendy tried to understand. He seemed to have a special insight into the animal, and a special horror of it. It had started out as just an experiment—one he was committed to, and one he was able to control. But now it was out of his hands. He had created something that might destroy him psychically. It had been building for weeks and it crystallized when he heard about Hall's mother. The thing that was happening to his animals and the thing that was happening in the city were truly linked in his mind. Not that it was so impossible.

Maybe the analogy could be useful. Maybe the city *was* like his enclosure. At least the idea might teach them something, direct them somewhere. Maybe she should talk to her father about it.

·16·

"Dad?"

"No." It was Francis. "He's in New Jersey."

"Why there?"

"A chemical company."

"How are they doing?" she asked.

"Coming along."

"What else do you know?"

"I'd rather not go into it on the telephone," he said.

"Who would be tapping *your* phone?" she asked.

He remained silent.

"Really," she said, "can you fill me in a little?"

"Why should I?" he asked. "What would you do with it?" The bitterness he felt toward her was unconcealed when their father wasn't on hand.

"Will you stop being an ass."

"That's the way you would see it."

"I only want to help, we've run across something that might be useful."

"And what would that be?"

"You won't talk, but I'm supposed to."

"There's nothing new," he said, reluctant even to say that. "Whatever you read in the papers is where it's at. They haven't got the chemical story yet, but it should be out in a couple of days. They traced it to a specific plant. Now what do you have to tell dad?"

"Are you sure that's all of it?"

"Would I lie to my own sister?"

"I've no doubt of that," she said, "but what I want you to tell him is that we have an idea that I think he should hear. Nothing concrete, but something interesting that comes out of my friend's research—"

"The Jewboy? The smart old Jewboy?"

"Cut it out, you son of a bitch."

She could hear him laugh. "And what does that make you?"

"Francis, why are you such a pig?"

"Call me what you want," he said, "at least I don't live like you do, treating your body like a lending library, and I'm not buddy-buddy with people who belong to secret black armies and I don't have friends who torture animals—"

"I think you're getting a little carried away," she said. "I also don't know where you get your weird information."

"I have my sources. I know about them and I know all I have to know about you."

"You're working on fantasy."

"I know better. I know those people are capable of anything. I know they're capitalizing on these killings to start their own race war—"

"Right, as if they don't have you to start it on your own."

"I'm not a racist, Wendy. No matter what you think. No matter what you tell James."

"Is that what you think I tell him?"

"I know you're trying to influence him."

"I don't tell him the kind of stupid bullshit you concoct."

"I don't concoct anything. Do you deny that your black friend was a member of the Black Student Consensus?"

"I'm not on trial," she said. "What do you know about my 'black friend'? Which one are you talking about?"

"Don't be cute with me. I know more about your promiscuous life than you think. I intend to use it if I have to."

She could hardly talk. "Just give the message to dad." She was about to hang up.

"One thing," he said.

"Yeah?"

"If you really want me to stay out of your life, if you really want me to let you and your friends alone, well, all *you* have to do is stay away from James."

"Fuck you," she said, and hung up.

·17·

ED HALL WAS in the laboratory alone. His mother was alive. She had smiled up at him when they finally let him see her, the crisis past, a strong woman made vulnerable by her sometime visits with her family down south and her work in the tobacco fields.

Now it was Hall's turn to watch the animals. He had no desire to be there, would have preferred instead to be out searching for the killer, the white bastard who poisoned his mother, another in the line of bastards who had poisoned her before. He knew as soon as he thought of it how pointless that would be. There was nothing he could do, no special knowledge he had, no way of getting at the man. Besides, he owed the time to Goldenson. He turned on the radio and let the music come over the speaker softly as he smoked a cigarette. Finally, a minute before he was scheduled to begin, he went to the enclosure with a clipboard. In contrast with Goldenson, Hall treated his observations as just a job. There was no special thrill in it for him, no private payoff, no insight into his own unconscious. Nor was there a career in it. He had no desire to teach or conduct research. It was, quite simply, the way he earned his money, the way he kept himself in school, the way he paved his way for his eventual acceptance into medical school. And though there were certain aspects of the experiment that intrigued him—that might some day have human implications—he was able to keep his distance from it. This was true especially of the observation work. He got no pleasure out of sitting there passively. He found it boring, even if they were animals that copied people, or had people copying them. Despite his interest in psychiatry he saw himself as a man of action. He would never be the passive type, would use his knowledge to bring on social change.

At the precise moment when he was scheduled to begin, Hall peered into the enclosure. The scene was strangely different from before. The animals were exceptionally quiet. At first he thought it was because they had been alone for a day, unstimulated by any sounds from the lab, but he knew that wasn't a sufficient cause. He looked around the enclosure for Irving, the rat Goldenson had identified, but was unable to locate him. Many of the other rats looked peculiar: some were asleep with their mouths wide open, some looked dead, and some were wandering aimlessly as if they were blind. At first he wondered it they had been struck by a disease. Then he thought that they had been poisoned, as though the killer outside had put parathion in *their* food, and he looked automatically in its direction. The food was untouched. But now, in the same glance, he saw the problem—they were out of water. The trough was empty, and the long plastic tube that brought water in from a tank on the wall outside was empty as well. He walked around the enclosure to the large plastic container and saw that it was dry. It was all very peculiar . . .he had checked it himself a few days ago and there had been at least a week's supply.

He filled a pail of water from the sink and carried it to the container. For a fraction of a second he had the impulse to deny it to them, to become their executioner, but he stifled the feeling—it was not his decision to make—and poured the water in. He could see it run into the tube and then begin to fill the trough. When the trough reached the right level, almost to the top, the flow stopped. From then on it would regulate itself automatically, additional water trickling in as it was needed. That was how it should have worked before. And as soon as the first drops of water flowed into the trough the rats crowded around to drink. Soon every animal in the enclosure that was still able to move was fighting to reach the liquid. Hall watched the scene impassively. There was a part of him that compared them to a mass of starving refugees in some overcrowded country. It made him think of what was happening in parts of Africa, of what had happened in Biafra and East Pakistan.

There was another side of him—the side that was in control—that rejected that line of thought and saw it as a kind of pit into which it was dangerously easy to fall. Goldenson was filled with that kind of subjectivity. He needed to keep his objectivity if he were to help the explosive kids and others he worked with. The result was—he knew it sometimes but avoided the thought —a kind of rigidity, an over-objectivity that made him seem unspontaneous, nothing at all like what he felt inside.

Now Hall studied the inside of the enclosure. Irving was nowhere to be seen. But when the crowd at the trough thinned out the rat did appear. He had been on the floor beneath the window at which Hall was sitting, in a place where he couldn't be observed. Now he made his way slowly across the floor and directly to the trough. Finally, he drank too. He apparently had suffered from dehydration like the others. When he'd had his fill he paused, and with the directness that had become typical of him he placed his body beneath the lip of the trough. Straining with all his might he managed to lift one corner. The water poured onto the floor of the enclosure and soaked the sawdust. The excess went down the drain that was there for cleaning purposes. As the trough lightened he lifted it higher, and now the water flowed directly from the tube, unregulated by any back-pressure, over the low edge of the trough and onto the floor. He remained immobile as the water came pouring out. In a few minutes the reserve was again empty. When the flow stopped Irving released the trough. He drank the few drops that remained inside, then made his way up the ramp and back to his special shelf.

The animal seemed unusually subdued, unusually focused, and Hall began to feel that it knew quite well what it was doing. What else was there to think? He began to believe that he had witnessed a conscious act of destruction. For a while he just sat there, trying in some way to absorb what he had seen. His boredom, his reluctance to engage in the task, were gone. There was no escaping the thought of connection with the deaths outside . . . the connection between his mother and this mass of victims. For a long time he looked at them, not making the notes that were expected of him, as the animals went about their normal activities. The dead were inspected and eaten. The females in heat were pursued by groups of males and mounted repeatedly. The nursing mothers on the floor continued to look for and sometimes find their wandering and doomed offspring. Life went on as it always went on, in a grotesque equilibrium, with no sign in the midst of it that one rat was committed to the complete destruction of the others, and that he was succeeding.

Hall looked in on them as if for the first time. All the violence he had seen before took on a new meaning, became more painful to him. He worried about the victims. It was too early for the rats to be harmed by the new absence of water, but he decided to provide more anyway. Before leaving the window he activated the movie camera. Then he filled the pail again, to the top this time, and brought it to the water tank. As soon as he filled the tank he returned to the window. The new supply made no immediate difference because the rats had had their fill, but Irving was already moving slowly down the ramp. Hall watched, unbelieving, as Irving repeated the movements he had made before—this time, at least, he had it all on film. In a short while the water was gone again. He refilled the tank. He had the feeling now that it was a contest between the rat and himself, the forces of death against the forces of life, and as he poured the water in he smiled in the firm conviction that he couldn't lose.

Again Irving emptied the trough.

It now occurred to Hall that there was a simple way of defeating the animal. He stepped away from the window. "I'll see you later," he said aloud. He searched the lab and found two strips of pliable metal and a hammer and nails. When he returned to the enclosure a few minutes later Irving was back on his shelf. Hall smiled, caught up in the struggle in a way he would never have believed. His objectivity was gone. He pushed the door open and entered the enclosure. The smell was as intense as ever, and the animals darted away, but he hardly noticed them. He kneeled beside the trough and placed the metal strips across each end. Then he nailed each strip to the floor. He tugged once and was satisfied. It was immobile now. To teach the animal a real lesson he might electrify the metal strips, but he felt that would be going too far. His urge to frustrate the rat was overwhelming. He might already have gone too far, lost too much distance from the situation, but he felt confident that Goldenson would approve. His first act, when he was outside, was to switch the camera on again. Then he refilled the tank with cool fresh water.

The rat was slow to come down. Perhaps, Hall thought, he had already had enough. Perhaps Hall's presence had disrupted him. But then he did begin to move. He sniffed for several seconds at the metal strips, but apparently failed to grasp their significance. He wasn't *that* smart. Soon he placed his shoulder against the trough again and attempted to lift it. When it failed to budge he gathered his energies for a second heave, and this time, as he sustained the effort, his eyes bulged and his mouth sagged open.

"Bust a gut, you little white bastard," Hall said aloud. He read shock and dismay in the animal's expression. Irving again tried to budge the trough. He strained for several seconds against the strip, his eyes bulging again, his mouth open and his tongue hanging out, and for all the world, to Hall, he looked human. Like a pitiful demented bastard, was Hall's angry thought. And he did succeed in jarring the trough slightly, having lifted it perhaps an eighth of an inch, but it was insufficient; the task was clearly too much for him.

Now Irving backed away from the trough and began to circle it, as if searching for another alternative. Then he approached again, climbed over the edge and into the water, and raised himself on his hind legs. He leaned against the tube but was unable to budge it. He gnawed the plastic, but was unable to penetrate it. Then he began to splash wildly, expelling the water from the trough. The level remained the same—it filled itself automatically. He continued to splash for several minutes, but it failed to satisfy him and he stopped and remained motionless in the water. "Freeze, you motherfucker," Hall said aloud. The rat looked uncomfortable, its fur matted, the colors on its back more difficult to see. Soon its body began to tremble. "Freeze your white ass off," Hall said. Then, realizing what was happening to him, he shook his head from side to side. He was being ridiculous. He had gotten caught up in the thing as if he was responding to an actual person. Now he felt embarrassed and annoyed. He sat there watching, trying to get back into his old control as the rat left the water. When it was gone he could see that it had defecated there.

·18·

THEY MET LIEUTENANT MCGHIE in a midtown bar. Goldenson
had come reluctantly. It was a meeting he had long anticipated
and long hoped to avoid. Now at least they had something to
talk about besides his relationship with Wendy, though in truth
he would have preferred the other issue. They shook hands and
looked into each other's eyes as Wendy made the introduction.
She knew the distaste her father felt for Goldenson, but she
knew also his willingness to explore any possible lead. McGhie
took his drink from the bar and led them to a table in a quiet
corner of the room. "So you know the answer," he said when
they were seated.

"I never said that," Goldenson carefully replied.

"Well, you said something, that you knew something—that
you had an idea, which is more than we have at the present moment." It was obvious that he had been drinking for more than
a little while.

"Nothing?" Goldenson was surprised.

"We have information," Lieutenant McGhie said. "No
ideas. At least no good ideas." He leaned forward across the
table. "That's what we need you intellectuals for."

They tried to ignore the bitterness. "What information do
you have?" Wendy asked. "Can you bring us up to date?"

"I'm telling you this in confidence. They traced the poison to
a plant in Jersey. It all comes from the same place. They lost
two hundred gallons of it six months ago. Someone carted it

out of the warehouse. They kept quiet because they were afraid of publicity. Rotten bastards. Figured it was some tomato farmer out to improve his crops. What the hell, they probably figured a little more in our salad won't do any damage. It was labeled carefully enough—that's all they cared about. There are no controls. They didn't do anything illegal." He sipped his drink. "And the plumbing equipment. We had a record of that one, although nobody put it together with parathion. It was taken from a supply house in Brooklyn. Someone backed a truck up against a window and hauled it away. It'd been tagged a family job, some hungry bastard in the business."

He sipped his drink again and studied them. There was a weariness in his face, and genuine despair. "The department is following up on every theft of every object that could conceivably be used to spread the stuff. But it's hopeless. We're stretched too thin. There are just too many possibilities. There's a hundred thousand junkies in this city stealing and selling everything that isn't nailed down. That's a lot of action we could do without." He signaled the waitress for a round of drinks. "And it's not as if our friend has a pattern—at least not yet. The bastard has hit four times in four different ways: the food, the pool, the movie, the drinking water. We have to assume he'll do it differently again. He's still a beginner. That stuff is so damn lethal he can deliver it in any of a million ways and wipe out half the city. It's as good as nerve gas in the strength he has it."

He looked Goldenson in the eye again. Every trace of drunkenness had disappeared. "So you know why I'm here," he said. "Because I owe it to my daughter and because I respect her judgment. I know she wouldn't call me for nothing. I also like to know the company she keeps. So tell me what's on your mind."

Wendy looked annoyed. "I told you about Solomon. I also told you not to expect anything specific."

"Yeah. You're a professor, right? They're never specific."

"He's an experimental psychologist," she said.

Goldenson cleared his throat. He would use his best academic voice. Under other circumstances he might make jokes, relax the atmosphere, but now there was just no time. It was his first excursion outside his lab in weeks and the world still felt a little strange. His mood was calm, subdued, still trancelike. He would try to be as clear and unspectacular as possible. "The situation, Lieutenant McGhie, is that I've been doing research on the effects of overpopulation, the effects of intense crowding. There's a phenomenon I've observed—it isn't unique to my research—that Wendy and I thought you might want to know about. Briefly as possible, it goes like this. When the population density in a community of animals reaches a given point, and persists at that point for a given period of time, the animals usually take it on themselves to bring things back into line. Some of them become overtly destructive, or self-destructive. Others become maladaptive. The net effect is that the birth rate declines and the death rate goes up."

"And you think people do the same?" McGhie jumped to the point.

"In a way," said Goldenson. "But not quite. What I've described isn't specific enough. Don't you want me to be specific? If you counteract the rat's maladaptation, if you keep the birth rate high and the death rate relatively low through artificial means, so that they have to contend with the crowded environment over a long period of time, with the most adaptive reproducing and the least adaptive dying young, then something new begins to happen. There are two dimensions to it. One is the effect on organisms already living in an overcrowded environment; the other is the effect of the environment in fostering the survival and reproduction of particular organisms. A psychologist named Milgram, right here in the city, studied the first kind of thing—remember that Kitty Genovese woman—the fact that most people in a crowded city just learn to tune things out. It isn't simply that they don't care. There's just too much going on and everyone deadens himself a little, ignores a lot of powerful stimuli—has to do it in order to survive. A biologist named Calhoun studied the effects of crowding on a larger scale. He observed all kinds of bizarre and destructive behavior that appears to be the result of crowding. My own work has extended his. As far as I can tell, if you keep the crowded conditions going long enough, you get an entirely new breed of animal."

"I get the drift," said McGhie, but he was obviously becoming impatient, even irritated. Unlike Goldenson's students, he didn't have to worry about an exam.

"You produce a new creature," Goldenson said. "Not a new species, at least not yet, just a rat, but one who behaves in a very special way. You get an animal with only one purpose in life—to destroy the others, and he does it with enough ingenuity to put your poisoner to shame."

"So you think you have a rat-size edition."

"I tried to avoid it. I'm not in the habit of thinking that way," said Goldenson. "I prefer not to extrapolate. Quite often it doesn't hold up. But I thought, given the circumstances, that you might want to know. Wendy thought you would want to know." He felt incongruous there, with his unkempt hair and sloppy clothes and his conservative and cautious speech.

"And if you did let yourself think that way?"

"In some ways rats are remarkably like human beings. In some ways, much more than monkeys. After all," he said, with his shoulders hunched forward and a gleam in his eyes, "people and rats share the same environments—houses, sewers, slums. Monkeys live in the jungle. What do they know about the city? What do they know about pollution, except for a few unfortunates in zoos?" He couldn't help smiling. "What do they know about technology? The rat has shown an ability to adapt to technology rivaled only by man and the cockroach, and we can't possibly consider the cockroach here because his nervous system is entirely different, though he does respond to parathion similarly. . . ."

Goldenson tried to restrain himself. He didn't want to come on like the mad scientist. He suspected that everything about him offended McGhie. He sat up straighter now and then went on. "Still, it's always risky to generalize from any lower animal to man. Most of the popular books that try to do it are pure fantasy. Language and symbol formation are such a jump from the intellectual processes of lower animals that there is just no way to translate their experience into ours. Often something that seems on the surface similar turns out to be entirely different when you examine it in detail—"

Wendy broke in. "What he's trying to say is that he doesn't have very much confidence in this whole thing. You know I pushed him to meet with you. He would rather beat around the bush and qualify everything with nine million alternatives instead of coming to the point and telling you what his guts are telling him." She was annoyed and showing it. "You see, despite his freaked-out looks, despite his peculiar habits, deep down inside him he's a true professor." She looked at Goldenson angrily.

McGhie nodded. It was almost as if he had stepped into a domestic quarrel. Who would have thought it of his liberated daughter? "Let me ask you this. What if your speculations were all correct? What could you tell us about the killer? Do you have any idea where we should look? Can you speculate about the kind of person we should look for, the kind of thing he may try next?"

Goldenson finished his drink and waved for another. Things had taken an uncomfortable turn. He found himself reluctant to talk about his ideas. He didn't want McGhie to know. It was more than caution. It was as if there was a part of him that wanted to protect the killer. "Don't look for a grudge," he said finally. "That would be irrelevant. Nor a psychotic. Look for an ordinary person. Probably a man. I would guess he came from a large family," Goldenson went on. "Or an orphanage. Something like that. A crowded steet, a crowded city. I would say that he had to feel hemmed in all his life, encroached upon."

"Well, in New York, that would cut the possibilities down to about one in six million," McGhie said. He had no intention of revealing that at least in one respect the description jibed with that given by the landlord.

"The urge to do it was not something that just came over him," Goldenson went on. "He had the fantasy throughout his life. He probably did things that expressed it before, though maybe in disguised ways. It took him time to get to the place where he is at. He had to learn to do it. He had to feel his way. I would guess that if one could examine his life one might find this sort of special thread—that he feels the pressure of people, maybe he shows it in small ways, maybe he shows it in ways that are considered socially good . . ."

"You mean he worked for planned parenthood or does abortions?" Lieutenant McGhie asked. The sarcasm dripped from his question.

"It may not be that simple," said Goldenson. He smiled, just for himself, a combination of the alcohol and a private thought. "Maybe he worked to encourage people to reproduce so they would kill themselves much sooner. He could be a Catholic. . . ." It just slipped out, an isolated stab.

"You got me here for this crap?" McGhie asked Wendy as he began to rise. "I can do without it. Believe me, I have problems you don't even know about."

"Just listen," she hissed at him. "I knew it would freak you out. Just listen anyway." There was something in her tone that told him that if he walked away he might never see her again.

They turned to Goldenson and waited. Once again he had to try to say something meaningful. He had to pull it out of his unconscious like an impacted tooth. "I don't know what to tell you," he began. "I said I assume he got to where he's at quite gradually. Even the killings have that quality. He's become more and more effective as he's gone along. He's exploring methods. I assume he had to learn something about poison. He had to learn to see death as a solution. If I'm right in my first assumption, that he's no psychotic, it means he had to overcome a lot of other conditioning that told him that killing is evil. So I ask myself where he learns to kill? Where does a normal American boy, from a large but poor family, where he was taught to respect the law and authority . . . where does he learn to kill? Where does he learn to use poison? And I get an answer . . . the army."

Wendy looked at her father. She tried to touch his hand. She knew he would be thinking of Joseph, her missing brother.

But Lieutenant McGhie was icy calm. "So you think we should check out everyone who's been in the service."

"That's what it amounts to," said Goldenson. "I could be more specific and say the guys who learned to kill at a distance, the pilots, maybe the ones who sprayed defoliants. But given certain events, certain killings, I would wonder about everyone who was in the war."

"And you call yourself a scientist?" said McGhie. "You don't know the difference between your sick politics and your sick animals." He got to his feet and dropped a bill on the table.

Goldenson rose as well. "I know about your son. I'm not

trying to be cruel or insulting. I didn't propose this meeting."

McGhie looked at Wendy. "You should have known better," he said before he left.

·19·

"HE'LL HAVE TO come up with something else," said Goldenson.

"Like what?" Wendy asked.

"I wish I knew."

Hall told them about Irving's attempt to deprive the others of water. "I just wish," said Goldenson, "that I had been here."

"Maybe he'll try again," said Hall. "Or you can wait a week, till they process the film."

"He won't do it again," said Goldenson. "He never does the same thing twice. And I'm not so sure we have a week." He turned to Wendy: "I suppose we should call your father. Or you should call your father. Maybe this would convince him. Maybe he would see that there is some weird kind of parallel."

She went to the telephone and called Lieutenant McGhie. "Dad?" Her eyes were closed as she listened. "Will you let me talk?" She spoke softly, though with great tension in her voice, and the urgency of the call apparently got through to him. Neither had expected that they would speak again so soon. "The animal went after the water. Do you understand what I mean? It went after the water. It tried to kill the others by leaving them with nothing to drink." She was silent now as he replied. "I *know* it's farfetched. I know it could be a coincidence. I know it's a long shot and that you find the whole idea distasteful. I know what you think of him. But it also could mean something important. Who really knows? Maybe the phenomenon, or whatever it is, takes similar forms. God knows, what else do you have to go on?" She listened again as he spoke and then abruptly said, "Okay, goodbye."

Now she turned to Goldenson and Hall. "He appreciates the call. I don't think he believes a word of it, but he appreciates the call. He said if anything else happens I should call him again. If we come up with something specific, I should call him again."

"Is he going to do anything?" Hall asked.

"Not now. If he told anyone they'd take him off the case. They're more uptight than he is. He doesn't have that much power."

Goldenson sadly shook his head. "So we have to wait for another disaster. Three hundred bodies don't quite add up."

"He said he would try," said Wendy. "He can't do much. He'll put someone on the Vietnam thing, to check out your theory, if he gets the chance. He isn't calling the shots."

Goldenson shrugged. "I suppose it's some progress. He must be as scared as I am."

There was nothing for them to do now but think again about the situation, try to explain it somehow. As usual, it was Wendy who pushed the questions.

"That defeats the interference theory," said Goldenson. "Or at least one aspect of it. It isn't enough to say that the interferences are random." Hall already knew his thinking, but he explained himself for Wendy's benefit. "We used to talk—other experimenters have talked—about the disruptive consequences of social stimulation. When there are more animals they are forced to engage in much more social contact. These interactions are normal and compelling for most animals—they're related to sex and dominance and territoriality. They're the essence of life. And these interactions are necessary in the normal life cycle of the animal. It has to have these contacts. It learns from them, its behavior is channeled by them. This is all well and good in the normal environment—the animal responds when the situation demands it, in the way that the situation requires, and it's possible to survive and to raise offspring satisfactorily." He turned toward the enclosure for a moment. "But when you force them to have more social contacts—forget about everything else—you find that they have disruptive effects, that they begin to interfere with other things. The social interactions become more dominant than the particular activity, even a biologically necessary activity, that the animal is engaged in. So you get the mother—you remember—who abandons her litter because she's having social contacts with a lot of other animals. Or the rats that won't eat unless they're in the middle of a crowd."

"The speculations of a recluse," Wendy said.

"Not just mine," he said, and smiled, but he was thinking that maybe she had a point. "It's in the literature. But it's not the whole story. That's what I see now. It's not the whole story . . . it doesn't explain enough." He looked at Hall and went on. "The difficulty has been in going from *that* to the bizarre behavior. How do you explain tail biting on the basis of social stimulation? How do you explain the slashing attacks? Above all, how do you explain Irving? What we have to add to this is the mechanism of aggression. We have to talk about the specific effects of all this stimulation on the animals' aggressive potential."

He paused and looked at each of them. Now he was into things he had never discussed before. "Let me put it another way. We all agree that survival demands aggressive behavior. Not necessarily destructive—in fact, usually nondestructive—but still aggressive. That is, if you want to make it in this world you have to assert yourself. You have to learn to express your aggression appropriately, and other animals have to learn to respond to the signals of your aggression. You have to learn to tell people to get off your ass, and they have to learn when they really should and when they don't quite have to. What I'm working toward, what I think it might be possible to show, would be that in *this* environment that mechanism becomes disturbed. It would be like those monkeys that Harlow raised on artificial mothers made of terry cloth. The mothers were fine—soft, warm, and always there. And never aggressive. Not in the slightest way. So when the monkeys grew up they couldn't copulate. They weren't aggressive enough to screw, or they couldn't control the aggression involved. In this environment, I'm speculating, it becomes impossible for them to display all the aggression that gets stimulated by all the social interactions they have to engage in. They have to control it to a greater degree than normal rats, and they're finally forced to displace it in various bizarre ways." He became increasingly excited as he went on. "That would be the source of population control in nature. When too many creatures get together they're guaranteed to stimulate each other to the point where some will inevitably die. In other words, every species might have built into it a mechanism in which further social interaction sets off the kinds of responses that will reduce the population. In other words"—his eyes were open wide—"every community can be thought of as the equivalent of a quantity of uranium-235. When a critical mass is reached, when the creatures collide with each other to a sufficient degree, you get a big boom, or its equivalent, and the species has to start again from scratch, or in some cases, I imagine, less than scratch."

"I'm losing you," said Wendy.

"Let me say it another way." He paused and tried to organize his ideas. "Being involved in social interaction inevitably produces aggression. In a normal environment there are ways in which this aggression is expressed. Sometimes it can be communicated directly. Something stimulates it—remember that this is inevitable—and the aggression is released. Sometimes this is not possible, for various reasons, and the aggression can then be, as the Freudians say, displaced—shifted so that it comes out another way. It can also be contained. Anyway, I'm not concerned with all the subtleties right now. The point is, it doesn't destroy the animal's adaptive capability—in fact under most conditions it probably helps. That's roughly what I think might happen in a normal environment." He looked at her. "Okay so far?"

She nodded.

"Okay, now what I'm saying is that if you take this model and try to get it to work under conditions of serious overcrowding, it tends to break down. It can't hold up. The rat gets flooded with aggression as a result of all its interactions, but it has no way in which to express it fully. You get tail biting, uncontrolled attacks, the elimination of the kinds of patterns people used to call instinctive. You get random aggression, just like in the city. But even that isn't enough. I think, eventually, you get some kind of structural breakdown, some basic change in the nature of the organism. Irving is an example. . . ."

"No wonder you stay away from people," she said.

He looked at her angrily. "Don't play shrink with me." In fact her comment had been quite accurate.

Hall laughed out loud. "Why not, I think you need it. It's the most autistic theory I ever heard. I know you've heard of the law of parsimony. I remember once you gave a lecture on it— no unnecessary assumptions, no postulates that aren't required. And here you go talking about the buildup and inhibited discharge of some hypothetical aggression. It's a figment of your own unconscious. It's completely unnecessary. Why can't you talk about the disruptive effects of certain kinds of conditions without postulating all sorts of unnecessary and unverifiable mechanisms? Why can't you explain the behavior on the basis of what's happening, on the basis of the horrors these animals have to contend with, without assuming some kind of innate hypothetical mechanism? I'm surprised at you," he said to Goldenson.

"You know," said Goldenson—and the strain of his feelings was clearly on his face—"I could kill you." He picked up the hammer that was on the table—the hammer Hall had used to nail down the water trough—and for a moment looked as if he might throw it. "I really could. It would give me great pleasure right now, a tremendous release." He put the hammer back on the table. "Of course I wouldn't. I mean I assume you know I wouldn't, but I felt the urge. I was really flooded by the urge." He sat there silently for a minute as they watched him. "And you didn't do anything. At least not anything that warrants that. All you did was rub me the wrong way. All you did was assert yourself, which you're entitled to, a little more strongly than I might have liked. You moved into my territory. You tried to take over a part of my space. You crowded me, and in front of my girl."

Wendy now understood what he'd done—it was a way of trying to demonstrate his idea. He was trying to expose them to the forces that affected his animals. But of course there was no way of proving that. The whole incident was confusing. The only certain thing was that he had actually experienced those forces inside himself.

·20·

No one paid much attention when the insects began to die. The few species brave enough to make their homes in Greenwich Village—in that stagnant air, that lack of greenery—were not the sort whose disappearance caused anyone to mourn. One celebrated their passing with a private joy, a sense one might have been briefly favored by the Gods, that one had found, finally, a decent way to live. The last thing you were likely to do was brag that the roaches and bedbugs had left your apartment. And so the disappearance of these creatures—they weren't all dead, of course, they had just suffered a temporary reversal and better adapted strains would have soon enough appeared—remained a private matter. It was unfortunate that it was overlooked, because the change, signifying an alteration of considerable significance in the ecology of the area, might have alerted someone—if there had been someone to consider such matters—that something dangerous was happening. As it turned out no one noticed publicly, and the fact of their disappearance came out only when the event they signaled was reconstructed afterward.

The pigeons began to die on Saturday, another unfortunate coincidence—had it happened during the week there might have been someone from the Board of Health or the ASPCA to investigate. They died gradually, hardly noticeably at first, though at an accelerating rate throughout the day. At first they seemed only lethargic, so that the occasional child who chased after a flock in Washington Square found, to his great surprise, that he was able to catch them. Drivers noticed that the birds that foraged in the streets, usually so adept at dodging cars, had lost the sharp edge of their ability. By afternoon the pavements of the narrow streets near the Hudson River were strewn with the flattened carcasses of hundreds of dead birds. But except for those few strange souls who wandered the city with their bags of grain or bread looking for pigeons to feed, no one paid attention.

The first serious notice that birds were being killed by something other than the cars was made by those who kept flocks of homing and racing pigeons on the roofs of the tenements they lived in. Their rage at finding their coops full of dead and dying birds created an uproar of sorts in Little Italy that afternoon, but this too attracted insufficient general attention. Who were the pigeon owners supposed to complain to? Who cared?

It wasn't until after dark that the great mass of birds began to die, the "clinkers," the street pigeons, who were more hardy than those reared in the protection of the coops.

Whatever their resistance, eventually there were no birds alive in the western part of Greenwich Village. Had trained people been on the scene, had they had the appropriate equipment, had they thought about the implications for the people of the area perhaps it all would have turned out differently. As it was, no one suspected that parathion was again at work.

After the pigeons it was the cats and dogs—the huge number that populated the neighborhood—and then the people. The impact was subtle at first. Old people and those who had once been agricultural workers developed symptoms within the next few days. Their weak condition or their low level of cholinesterase made them especially vulnerable. But for most of the community the effects were slow and gradual. It seemed like a summer cold. People felt chilled, felt the aches and pains that might have, by this time, warned them that something more serious was on the way. But everyone felt it in isolation, as his or her own particular misfortune. Instead of panic, at least for a little while, they fought their symptoms in a kind of lethargy. They were fighting a pain from the deepest sleep. If they had been awake they might have thought of a way to fight it, but in the state in which they found themselves—in part produced by the poison—they could do little but roll aimlessly in private agony.

It was in the emergency rooms of Bellevue, Saint Vincent's, and Beth Israel hospitals that it became clear that something serious was happening. The death rate increased precipitously. Hundreds of people now appeared with breathing difficulties. Emergency calls went out across the city. It soon was established—the result of three rapid autopsies and a laboratory test—that the deaths were again due to parathion, this time concentrated in the victims' lungs. It took little imagination to go from that to the realization that the poison was suspended in the stagnant air. It was like the deadly fog that not so long before had descended on the city of Milan.

They tried hard to keep it quiet, but half the doctors left at once. Members of a medical team would be working feverishly, doing everything possible for the stream of people that was now arriving, seemingly indifferent to the possibility of being affected themselves, and then they would disappear. Perhaps it was in response to some minor symptom they perceived in themselves, perhaps it was a fear that when the news came out they would be unable to escape the city. Whatever the reason, they were there one minute and gone the next, without a word to anyone, sometimes in the middle of a vital task, one a patient's life depended on. Someone would go for oxygen and never return, in one instance carrying a small emergency tank of oxygen with him. And then it was into the car, the windows closed and the air conditioner turned up full, and out of the city as fast as possible.

The police and the doctors and the mayor met. The governor was on his way. The meteorologists informed them that there was no real hope for a wind—the city's air was unlikely to move for at least the next two days. Preliminary data revealed traces of parathion in every sample of air south of a line across Manhattan at about Fourteenth Street. There was no alternative to a massive evacuation. They would clear out the city below Twenty-third Street. There would be chaos, but they might save some lives. They would call in the National Guard. If they moved quickly there might be hope—the concentration in the air was not yet lethal unless breathed for an extended period. And so the call went out in English, Spanish, Yiddish, Italian,

Polish, Russian, and Chinese; on sound trucks, on the radio, and on the television screen. People were told to take their valuables, to lock their apartments, to leave as rapidly as possible. Things were not dangerous yet, there was time to get out, and food and emergency shelter would be available in Central Park. Looters would be shot by a special group of gas-masked police.

They came in wide streams up the avenues in what, from a great height, might have seemed like the advance of a colony of army ants. At closer range there was panic in the crowd, and confusion, but also some humor and even a sense of strength. They were all under the same attack, comrades in it together, like the London blitz, and there was comfort in that feeling, protection in numbers. They walked up the avenues, without buses or automobiles, without the usual fumes, just the gray smoke from the electricity generating plants and the puffs of white from the roofs of some isolated buildings. It might even have seemed festive had it not been for the fact that there were people in desperate trouble.

And though, for the most part, things remained calm, there were also moments of great cruelty and terror. When someone fell, usually an old person suffering from the effects of the poison and the stress of the evacuation, trembling, gasping for more of the poisoned air, they were treated as if their illness were contagious. If it had been a medieval city they might have burned the body. But in this city, at this time, they just avoided it. They relied on the tactic they all had learned, the tactic that made life in the city possible: look away. The crowd would split into separate streams and pour around the corpse. People held their breath. Others crossed themselves. No one stopped to help the victims . . . an ambulance would be there soon . . . the thing was catching . . . don't touch . . . don't get involved!

But nevertheless the city proved itself. The virtues of its people and its technology prevailed. Almost miraculously, within the space of hours, the streets and apartments of lower Manhattan were emptied. The park filled. Relief poured in. Atmospheric monitoring equipment was set up. The experts pronounced the rest of the city safe. It would continue to be as long as the air remained stagnant, as long as the wind did not blow from the south. Medical care was provided those who needed it. Emergency food supplies were rushed in. A city of tents came into being. For many, especially the children, it was an environment far more attractive than the one they had been forced to leave.

The police took to helicopters to survey the evacuated area. From the air the answer was obvious. Six buildings, in a kind of circle, several hundred yards from each other, puffed an oily white smoke from their chimneys. The smoke sat there, barely dissipating, sinking slowly down to the streets in a slightly less concentrated form. They radioed the locations into headquarters and soon six groups in gas masks and protective clothing made their way into the area, against the stream of refugees. Each group discovered that its target was unoccupied; either a tenement or a factory awaiting renewal. Their guns were drawn as they crashed through the doors, but they found no one. Instead, in the basement of each building, they found a battery-driven air compressor. Attached to each was an agricultural spray gun, with its output directed up the chimney and its input connected to a tank of parathion.

With the flip of a switch, the deadly spray stopped, but it would take at least two weeks before the area could be inhabited again.

·21·

IRVING CLAWED and bit at the wall of the enclosure.

"Does he have a chance?" Wendy asked. "Could he ever get out?"

"No way," said Goldenson. "If he does we're all in trouble. That wood is half an inch thick."

"We *are* in trouble," she replied.

Following his unsuccessful attempt to deprive the others of water Irving had sulked on his platform for several days, hardly showing himself. Then, abruptly, he reappeared, looking similar to the others in size and bedraggled condition. His defeat had shriveled him. It was only the red and blue on his back, slightly paled now but still clearly visible, that enabled them to distinguish him. He seemed to have joined the colony. His behavior took on the aimless, overly social quality that was so characteristic of the others. They began to wonder if he would just fade away. Could he have lost the power that made him so destructive and so invulnerable? But they saw, soon enough, that whatever pushed him to kill had not exhausted itself. Now Irving reverted to the style of his earliest attacks. He killed the others one by one. His assaults were so well accomplished, so intrinsically a part of the life of the colony that except for their effects they were hardly observable. He lived exactly like the others, ate their food, drank the water, spent his time as they did. The difference was that at least a dozen times a day, sometimes more often, he struck out and killed another animal. The population inside the enclosure continued to shrink. The normal death rate was always high, especially among the younger rats, but now it was skyrocketing. Every morning when he cleaned the cage Goldenson found the half-eaten carcasses of at least a dozen rats. Many carcasses he never found. At first they were puzzled. It was difficult to know exactly how the animals died. But when they watched Irving's every motion, his attacks became quite clear. Periodically he would sieze another rat from behind, bite deeply into the back of its neck, and tug once—once was enough—at its spine. Then he would leap off as the animal crumpled, already paralyzed, and continue his own activities as if nothing unusual had taken place. It was the ultimate refinement of the tail biting they had observed so many weeks ago: a highly practiced action, obscenely beautiful in its grace and speed, devastating in its effectiveness. Through a lucky break they had managed to film it in slow motion.

"I'll put a screen outside that corner," said Hall. "Just in case." Irving had been gnawing at it for the past three hours and there was now a visible depression in the wood.

Hall took a sheet of wire mesh and stapled it to the wall. Even if Irving did chew his way through the wood, he would never make it through the metal. But the rat did not break through, nor even seriously attempt it. After making a bit more progress on the wall he stopped abruptly and wandered off again among the other animals.

"Watch out," Goldenson muttered, and shortly thereafter he killed two more.

The population was down to one hundred adult rats and several litters. One thing was certain: the babies would have a better chance. If Irving stopped his assaults for any length of time the population would soon recover. But that possibility was never to be examined, because Irving began to kill more rapidly. At times he leaped from the back of one victim to the back of another. He became more frenzied and less accurate in his efforts now, as if the complete destruction of the colony excited him. Some animals were able to escape from him before the fatal bite. What now developed in the enclosure—Goldenson saw it first, as usual, and the others confirmed it—was a fear of Irving. It was the first indication that the rats had indentified him. Now when he approached another animal with some social gesture, it was likely that the animal would flee. When he tried to join a group, as he had in the past, he found that they refused him. At times they grouped together and made threatening gestures in order to drive him off. But it was clear that these efforts were in vain. Rats weren't capable, Goldenson explained, of sustained group defense. They were unable to protect themselves against Irving's assaults for any length of time. Soon their numbers were reduced to fifty adults, then thirty, with two newborn litters dying soon after their mothers were killed. Compared with a normal environment the enclosure was still overcrowded, but it looked almost deserted to the observers and they found themselves increasingly upset as the deaths went on.

It was as if, Wendy pointed out, they were watching the end of the world, and the feeling grew among them that this indeed was the way it would end—not in the explosion that always seemed so imminent. They found themselves numbed by the experience, and yet unable to tear themselves away from it, absorbed in it and tormented by it as Goldenson alone once had been. By now the three of them were living together in the laboratory. They were waiting for the inevitable end, eager for it, eager to conclude their work, and yet more gloomy as the moment approached. They became aware that they felt something like affection for the animals that they had housed and studied, even more than affection, a kind of love, perhaps a love of life, a love of anything that could be born and stay alive. In a way though none of them mentioned it—it occurred to each of them that in the death of the colony they were feeling their own imminent deaths, and perhaps even the death of the larger colony outside.

And finally the colony did reach its end. One morning there were only Irving and six other males. Goldenson removed the bodies of the animals that had died—all violently—during the night. He swept the droppings out—an easy job now. He had the distinct image—perhaps it was a wish—that he was visiting an alien planet. Soon he would step back into the spaceship that would take him away. He was an explorer who had found a grotesque new world inside the enclosure. He had observed it, participated in its life, felt its temptations, touched its horror.

He had been initiated into its mysteries, and they had touched the deepest part of him. Now it was time to break away.

Goldenson could see Irving watching him. He was careful to position himself between the animal and the door. He felt an uncomfortable tingling at the back of his neck. He had an image of Irving leaping off the floor and sinking those long and curved and pointed fangs, which had been dipped in so much blood, into his own skin and vertebrae. It was an unbearable sensation, unbearable in its pain and in the alarming, outrageous realization that it was tinged with a sort of, yes, sexual pleasure. An erection thrust up in him like an uncoiling spring. He doubled over, in pain and embarrassment and confusion, then quickly left the enclosure, slamming the door behind him. Fortunately the feeling subsided.

"Are you all right?" Wendy asked.

"I think so." He took a seat at the window. He had to look at Irving again.

She seated herself beside him and wrapped an arm around him. "It's painful for you to be in there with him."

"More and more," he said.

They watched Irving leap on another animal. When a second rat approached to sniff the carcass, Irving quickly killed it. By afternoon, as they sat at the window, only one other animal was alive, a sick and terror-stricken creature that leaned and trembled against a wall.

Irving approached.

"The stupid bastard is offering his neck," Hall said.

"What else is there to do?" asked Goldenson.

"Fight the motherfucker."

"I wish I could," said Goldenson.

The others heard his unconscious slip but chose to let it pass.

"At least he could damage him," said Hall. "Make him pay a price."

Irving leaped on the other rat. It offered no resistance. When the fangs went into its neck it tried to pull away. All it succeeded in accomplishing was snapping its own spine.

"Bastard," said Goldenson.

Now Irving walked slowly around the floor of the enclosure. He might have been making certain that there was nothing else inside the place that was alive. When he was satisfied, he returned to the place where he had gnawed the wood. His movements increased in speed. He scratched and chewed at the wall and managed to tear large splinters loose with almost every bite. The more progress he made the more frenzied he became. The observers felt frozen. It seemed as if there was something about the enclosure that was now intolerable to him. He was using every bit of his energy in the effort to get out. "I think he's lonely," said Goldenson. "I think, all of a sudden, he misses them. He wants to find another place to live."

Soon blood appeared on Irving's claws, but it had no effect on his rapid work. Large chunks of wood came loose. They could hear, from their own side of the enclosure, the scratching grow louder. The wood between Irving and them was paper thin. They could hear the faint grunting sounds he made as he worked. Goldenson crouched beside the enclosure, his ear almost touching the wall. A claw penetrated the wood. Soon it became a small hole. In a moment Goldenson was face to face with the rat. All that separated them were the strands of the wire screen. He could look directly into the animal's eyes, hear and feel his breathing. He could see the pointed fangs as the rat tugged at the metal. They looked at each other. For one unbearable moment Goldenson felt that he was falling under Irving's power . . . under his spell.

"Ugly little bastard," Ed Hall said. "Something strange about his eyes."

Goldenson turned away.

Irving ripped at the screen. Now his mouth began to bleed.

"Tough break, old man," said Hall.

As if Irving heard, he backed away. He retreated to the far side of the enclosure, where he licked his paws. His bleeding soon stopped. For a long time he remained motionless. Finally he drank some water. Then very slowly, as if he was in pain, he climbed the ramp and returned to his old perch.

"No way out, old man," Hall said. "You have to live with what you've done."

·22·

WENDY WAS ON THE TELEPHONE with her father: "I can't do that," she said.

"You're being foolish. We're not any closer," Lieutenant McGhie said. "The only sane thing is for you to get out. I'd leave myself if I didn't have to worry about my pension."

"I believe you. But I can't go now. We're in the middle of something and I have to see it through. Maybe in a couple of weeks. I'll think about it in a couple of weeks."

Her father paused. When he began again, his speech was slow and measured. "God knows what will be in a couple of weeks. God knows if anything will be. We were lucky the last time. He miscalculated. It wasn't as bad as it might have been. He won't make the same mistake again."

"Can't you at least interfere with him?" she asked. "I know you can't find him, but isn't there some way you could slow him down?"

"We're trying that," he said, a tone of weariness in his voice. "We're organizing people. We hope to have inspectors on every block."

"That should do something."

"I don't know. Remember what your boyfriend said—he could even be one of us." He paused, still annoyed with the idea. "I think he's too smart to be affected much by our silly obstacles. Everything he does is too damn well planned. We've never had to deal with something like this before. We have no experience. We don't know what to look for next. It's a new ball game. The only thing we're certain of is that he'll hit again."

"I know," she said.

"We're trying to interfere with his ability to move the stuff around. We're searching cars and packages at random, trying to make it impossible to transport the stuff."

"But it takes so little of it to kill."

"I know that," he said irritably. He paused again. "I want you to know my thinking. I want you to know where we're at. The one thing we are sure of is that he's got less on hand than he did before. We figure he's down to forty or fifty gallons. His last little fiasco was pretty wasteful of the stuff."

"Only forty or fifty gallons," she repeated sarcastically.

"There are guards at every manufacturing plant in the country. I think it would be safe to say he won't get his hands on any more."

"What about other methods?" she asked. "What about other poisons? What about the one they thought was used in Philadelphia?"

"Do your father a favor and don't remind him."

"Well if he's that limited," she said, "it'll have to affect his approach." She paused and thought awhile. "When our rat was defeated in one way he tried something new."

"What was that?" he asked.

"He went back to killing individually."

"This bastard has never done it that way. He won't look his victims in the face. We're expecting," he went on, "that he'll try a more efficient method. We think he'll look for a method that won't waste his supply.

"Like back to the food?"

"Something like that."

"But unlikely, because he's done it already."

"We're not ruling it out."

"What other possibilities?"

He hesitated. It was the real purpose of his call to her. That's what I'd like you to think about, maybe get your friend to think about. He seems to know about this stuff. Tell him there's a big reward."

She restrained her urge to comment on his turnabout. "Of

course we'll think about it, dad. If we come up with anything I'll let you know."

"One other thing."

"Yes?"

"I know you understand the need to keep our conversation quiet."

She paused for a moment and then spoke quickly. "If you feel that way, then why don't you get Francis to leave our telephones alone."

"He's still at that?"

"More than ever. He wants to blackmail me. He's looking for a way to keep me from James."

"I'll talk to him," he said. "There are limits to everything." His voice sounded even more fatigued than it had before.

·23·

GOLDENSON WAS in his laboratory, Wendy had left for the library, and Hall was somewhere in the street—most likely with his youth gang. It was a chance to be alone with Irving, and he had been looking forward to it from the moment the day before when Irving killed the last of the other rats. What he hoped to find was far from clear, for there was little to observe in the absence of the other animals. Nevertheless, there was something magnetic about the creature, and he made his way slowly and silently to an observation window. He placed himself opposite the corner where Irving had chewed his hole. He hoped to watch, without being noticed himself, how the animal dealt with the fact that its efforts to escape had been frustrated. Once again the rat had shown incredible intelligence and ingenuity, and Goldenson wondered what direction the animal's energies would move in next.

Irving was on the floor of the enclosure, just finishing a visit to the food tray. In the large empty space he looked utterly indistinguishable from a normal laboratory rat. When he finished his meal he withdrew from the tray and made a slow circle around the floor. He approached the place where his escape had been impeded and sniffed repeatedly at the screen. Goldenson wondered whether he could still make out the human smell. He slowly made his way along the side of the enclosure, his nose pressed into the right angle made by the wall and floor. He was obviously looking for another way out. He

111

traced almost the complete perimeter of the enclosure before he stopped. Then he began to scratch and chew at the wall again. He had apparently worked at the same place before.

"Determined bugger aren't you," Goldenson said aloud.

The rat stopped and peered around the enclosure. In the silence it heard his voice. Goldenson kept quiet now and in a few moments the rat began to scratch again.

"A little uptight, aren't you?" he said.

Irving stopped again and sniffed the air. Once more, after a pause, he continued his efforts.

"I could control you this way."

Now Irving ignored the sound.

"Bastard." Goldenson rapped the wood sharply with his fist. Irving backed away from the wall. He sniffed the air again, peering nearsightedly around the enclosure, attempting to locate his tormentor.

"I won't hurt you," Goldenson said. He studied the motionless animal. Already its claws were bleeding. It could never repeat its prior feat. Goldenson felt a kind of compassion as Irving returned to scratch the wall. His compassion was short lived. He slammed the wood again, this time with all his might. The rat leaped back three feet. He looked around the enclosure for a place to hide. He scooted up the ramp to his old perch. For several minutes he remained out of sight as Goldenson waited silently. At last Irving's head appeared beyond the edge.

"Don't be afraid," Goldenson said. "I'm just feeling a little crazy." That was exactly what he was feeling, and the fact that he verbalized it failed to provide him with enough control. He was experiencing waves of powerful, conflicting emotion. There was no clear direction to it. In fact each wave seemed to pull him differently. He was alternating between a kind of compassion for the animal, even a tenderness, and a deep, almost overwhelming hatred. At one moment he wanted to enter the enclosure and choke the rat in his hands, at another moment he wanted to cradle it in his arms and ask forgiveness for the things he'd done to it. He wished Wendy were there. Finally he walked around the enclosure. He stopped at the place where Hall had stapled the mesh and he looked into the empty space inside, and up at the rat. Irving peered down at him, no longer afraid. "Come here," he said, conscious of the fact that there was no glass between them.

Irving remained on his perch.

"I won't hurt you. I promise you that."

The animal remained immobile.

Goldenson placed his hand on the mesh and in one abrupt and powerful motion ripped it away.

Irving remained immobile.

"You dummy," Goldenson said. He walked away from the enclosure without looking back. "Your big chance," he said as he stepped into the center of the room. On the floor was a metal drain. He tugged at it with his hands but it failed to budge. He found a screwdriver, placed it under the edge and pried the iron cover up out of the floor. There was plenty of room for the animal, and plenty of places where the drain might take him; it fed into the sewers of New York. He seated himself as far as possible from the enclosure in a corner of the basement. "One hour," he said aloud. "Your big chance."

In much less than an hour Irving appeared at the hole. He sniffed its edges, where the screen had been, and looked around the room. With great caution he dropped to the floor. Goldenson sat paralyzed. He wanted to strike out at Irving, destroy him totally, every trace of him. But the rat looked so tiny there, so innocent, so helpless. Before he had the chance to act, Irving ran straight across the floor and down the drain. He was gone.

·24·

"THAT WAS BRILLIANT," Hall said, "really brilliant."

"So what now?" Wendy asked.

Three hours had passed and Goldenson was still sitting in the corner. They were all depressed, each feeling that the thing had ended prematurely. The others were stunned by the fact that Irving was gone. His release had been so unexpected, so pointless. It also left them without their link to the killer. Irving had come to seem the only way the killer's future moves might be anticipated, and now he was lost forever. No one even considered repeating the experiment. It would take too long and anyway they couldn't be sure if they could produce another one like him. They might even end up with something more horrible. They had come to hate Irving, had come to dread the need to watch his exploits, but now that he was gone they felt his loss, and they felt more fully the reality of the killer outside —where Irving had gone.

"We could have studied him," Hall said. "I shouldn't have interfered either. I lost my distance too. We all did."

Goldenson spoke, his voice a monotone. "I don't think it matters. I know it was crazy, I feel crazy, but what else was there to learn? He couldn't tell us if he was an accident or a law of nature. I guess we could have bred him, if he didn't kill the female, we could have studied his offspring. There would have been a career in it, a full professorship for sure." He shook his

114

head from side to side, still slightly dazed. "But I intend to skip that opportunity."

"You're not going to work on it?" Wendy asked.

"I'll write up what we've done, but that's the end of it. I have to get away."

"From the killer?" she asked. There were two of them out there now. "Is that getting to you?"

"From the city, myself, this monstrosity . . ."

"You don't have any more ideas about him? You can't guess what he's up to? You don't have any feeling for him . . . ?"

"I have too damn much feeling for him."

There was a loud rap at the door. Goldenson answered quickly and found himself face to face with three policemen. He was still somewhat disoriented, unable even to object as Wendy's brother Francis McGhie stepped into the room.

"Up against the wall, motherfucker," said Francis. There was a small, triumphant smile on his face.

"You're kidding," Wendy said. "Get out of here, and take your stupid friends—"

"Not kidding at all," said Francis. "We have authorization to search the premises, from the college president."

"On what grounds?" asked Hall.

"You'll find out soon enough, fella."

There was nothing to do but stand there silently as the policemen searched the room. Wendy was enraged. Hall looked particularly tense. He kept his mouth shut. Goldenson still looked confused.

"Where do you keep it?" Francis asked.

"Keep what?" asked Goldenson.

Francis smiled knowingly. "You know what."

"My God," Wendy said, "this is like some lousy TV script. Damn you, Francis, I'll *never* forgive you for this."

He looked at her. "You didn't really think I'd just stand by and—"

"You have nothing to say about my life."

"I'm not *saying* anything."

The other two policemen continued their search, working rapidly and systematically but failing to locate whatever it was they were hunting for.

"Why don't you save us all a lot of trouble and tell us where it is?" said Francis. "You wouldn't want us messing up your laboratory."

"It's too late, it makes no difference what you do," said Goldenson. "The work here is finished."

Francis stepped across the room to the desk and bookshelves. He put his hand on a shelf and swept a stack of papers to the floor. He stood on the papers. "Nothing there," he said. "Well, we'll just have to look someplace else." He stood beside the enclosure and looked in a window. "Torturing animals? Brainwashing college girls? Hey, professor, is that the way you get your kicks?" For a moment it looked as if he might enter, but then he moved away. He circled the room slowly as the others watched and waited in silence. At the far side of the room, with his back to them, he rummaged in a stack of papers. "Well, well," he said as he turned to them, smiling broadly now. "What have we here?" He held up a bottle. It contained a small quantity of crushed green leaf, obviously marijuana. "You come with me," he said to Goldenson. "The good doctor here is pushing or using. How old are you son," he asked Ed Hall.

"Old enough to know a setup when I see one."

"Is that so?" He looked at the other policemen. "I don't think these officers would agree."

Wendy's anger became uncontrollable. "You crazy bastard, don't you know what you're doing? Don't you realize we're your best hope or figuring out what the killer will be up to next—"

"Is that so?" Francis smiled again. "My brilliant sister and her mixed bag here are going to save us. Like hell . . ."

They led Goldenson to the police car and drove him to the station, where they placed him in a solitary cell. He was aware, of course, that they had neglected to file a formal charge, but in a way he was relieved to be in isolation. It felt completely different from the last time he was in jail. Then he'd had company. A dozen protestors arrested and jammed together. It had panicked him, made him almost faint. Now all he knew was silence. It was better than being booked and in the tank. He paced the floor; it was four quick steps from wall to wall. He touched the bars, turned, went back and forth again and again. It was deathly quiet in the little cell, as if it were the only place in the world, as if he were the only person. It offered everything he needed: total freedom for his thoughts, total control of his behavior. He tried to break away from such thinking. He was still wrapped up with the animal, thinking of himself as the animal. He should be trying to make a plan. Why had they brought him here? What were they really after? How could he best respond? The situation was serious. Why did they go to this trouble? What was the point of it? He knew he should be thinking about how to handle himself but he just couldn't focus. There was too much rushing through his head . . . the way he felt now that the rat was gone, the changes in himself . . . there was a new awareness of being different from the others, something he'd dimly felt most of his life, but now it was there explicitly, on the surface. For the first time ever it was possible to look at it and think about it. He wasn't like the others, not really . . . he was a new creation with laws unto himself and with a future all his own. . . . He'd been terrified of this idea, had fought it off for so many years—and there was much about it that was still terrifying. It was no accident that it came to him while he was in a cell. He had a kind of vision of another life, a life not like anything ever known. He'd have power, complete power. He had kept enough of his old politics to feel repelled by his thoughts, to feel they were grotesque and evil. But there was another side to it, one that also had elements of joy, and now that he was alone—contained—it was possible for him to allow himself to feel that joy. He would have total control. Short of that he would know what was inside himself. He would have total power over himself. God, he needed power over something.

•25•

"WHAT DO YOU know about him?" Francis asked.

"I have nothing to say."

"Do you think this is a game? You're in real trouble."

"Do you think I can do magic?"

"Magic or murder," Francis said. "An accomplice of the killer." He stepped beside the chair Goldenson was seated in and for a moment it seemed he was about to hit him. "If I catch you around my sister again I'll break you in little pieces and flush each one down the toilet you belong in."

"Is that another part of your work? Do you get *your* kicks by snooping on her?" Goldenson felt uncommonly free of fear.

Francis raised his hand, but a voice from behind Goldenson's chair said, "Stop it," before he could hit him.

"Tell us again," Francis asked. "How did you know?"

"You'd never understand. It's beyond you."

The police had identified the killer. Goldenson's guess had been correct. The landlord who rented the basement to the killer had picked his face out of a pile of photographs. He was absolutely positive. The man's history fitted almost exactly with Goldenson's prediction. The killer had been a pilot in Vietnam. He had flown a plane that sprayed defoliants. He had been trained in meteorology. He was an expert in the distribution of severely toxic substances.

"They doped him out there and he turned into a freak like you," said Francis. "You're probably his pusher now."

"They doped him here on the same bullshit they feed to you," said Goldenson.

"You stupid damn communist—"

"Is *that* the charge?" asked Goldenson. "Don't you think it's about time you let me know?"

"We haven't decided yet."

"All right, I'll take it from here." It was Lieutenant McGhie. "I want you out of here," he said to his son.

"Creep, you'd better damn well watch it," Francis said as he left the room.

Lieutenant McGhie offered Goldenson a cigarette, which he refused. They were alone.

"I want a lawyer," Goldenson said.

"Let's keep it informal for a little while."

"It isn't informal."

"You have to understand the strain we're under."

"You have a hard life."

"I told him to bring you in," said Lieutenant McGhie. "I didn't tell him how. You'll be released. My son acted stupidly. I hope you're willing to forget it. I know you tried to help. In fact you've helped us more than anyone. My son can't accept the truth. He's in a rage. His girl friend lives downtown. She got a dose. Not enough to kill her, but a dose. They're afraid it might have some effect when they get married and try to have a child."

"It might," Goldenson said.

McGhie was silent. They looked at each other.

"You could never understand this thing," said Goldenson. "You have a case you could never figure out. Not just a case, not just a killer, you're stuck with a future that's beyond you."

"I don't follow you."

Goldenson found that he now felt like talking. "You need a motive," he said bitterly. "So do most psychologists. You're hung up on purpose, intention, when it's completely irrelevant. Just think about the flow, the way life is organized, the social system. Don't look for someone with some big-deal articulated *reason*. The guy who did these things doesn't want more room in the subways or smaller crowds at the beach. He isn't crazy. God didn't tell him to do it, or even if God did, it doesn't matter. It's a mistake. He wasn't appointed by God, he was appointed by the city. He was appointed by the way we live. He's going to change it all, but he doesn't even know or care about it. He was just in line to do the job. It doesn't matter why he *thinks* he does it. His reasons are irrelevant. Nature appointed him. Evolution appointed him. The next guy who takes the trip will have another set of reasons. Maybe he'll have a philosophy that he can call his own. Maybe a new religion. Maybe a new kind of politics. It doesn't matter. Whatever the elaborations, whatever the justifications, the underlying reason will be the same. It will be rooted in biology, in the laws of evolution. Everything else will be an afterthought."

"Be more specific."

Goldenson looked annoyed. "I didn't come here as a volunteer, remember. If I had anything specific to say I would have gotten in touch with you. I'm only playing around with some ideas. I'm only showing off . . . or maybe just showing you up . . . you figure it out. . . ."

Lieutenant McGhie changed his tack. "I think you should know where we are. Maybe it'll give you some more ideas."

Goldenson waited.

"We went to see his family but they said he'd left six months ago. He's been peculiar for the last few years. He broke off from everybody. Told them he was sick of the city, that he was going west. He said he'd found some new kind of work. They think he's in California. We talked with all his brothers and sisters—eight of them—and we couldn't come up with anything. All we know is that he's on the loose and probably still in the city. We're watching them. We're hoping he may contact them, though God knows why. His youngest sister lives in lower Manhattan and her two children were injured in the last attack. Even they're not safe."

"Nobody is safe," said Goldenson. "You still don't understand. He's not a freak, he's a new phenomenon. He follows different laws. If you want to understand him, try to imagine someone from another planet."

"I'll never understand him," said McGhie. "I've seen my share of horrors, but this is one I just can't get a hold on. . . ."

"I'd like to see what he looks like," Goldenson said.

McGhie paused for a moment, obviously considering whether to go ahead, then extracted a small photograph from his jacket pocket and handed it to Goldenson. "This is strictly between us. The fact that we've identified the bastard is still a secret. If the press got hold of it we'd just deny it. I'm trusting you on this."

Goldenson appeared not to hear. He looked long and deeply into the face. He tried to feel the man in the same way he felt his animals. He tried to grasp the essence of the creature looking at him. After several minutes he looked up at McGhie. He had nothing to say. Whether the reason was something in himself or the fact that it was just a photograph remained unclear.

"Ordinary looking bastard, isn't he?" said McGhie.

The man in the photograph had looked blandly into the lens. His hair was dark, close cropped, and his jaw was firm. He was wearing a neat dark tie, a white shirt, a dark suit. His nose was straight and undistinguished and his ears were set against his head. His only feature of any distinction was his pale eyes, either gray or light blue, but the bored or bland or indifferent expression on his face cooled the interest that in another face they might have aroused.

"Looks like a computer printout," said Goldenson.

"Nothing to say about him? No ideas?"

"Not from this picture." Goldenson continued looking at the man. "This is a hard rat to identify"—he suppressed a smile at his own small joke. "It's the kind of face one never remembers."

"That's part of the problem," said McGhie. "They're afraid to release the picture. It's as nondescript as the sketch we made. They're afraid he'll be confused with someone innocent. We've had enough of vigilantes."

Once again Goldenson studied the face. "Seems like a dumb reason. This guy has killed hundreds. It would be worth the risk."

"So then he puts on a disguise. At least this way he doesn't know we're onto him."

"It still doesn't make sense," said Goldenson. Once again he examined the picture. "Where was this taken?"

"After he left the service."

"That's not what I asked."

"For a government job. He made an application."

Goldenson looked silently at McGhie.

"All right, I'll tell you. The son of a bitch once worked for the CIA. We've been pressured to keep it quiet. They want a chance to catch him first."

·26·

GOLDENSON RETURNED to his laboratory. He planned to put his things in order, assess the damage Francis had caused, throw out the carcasses that still remained in the refrigerator and send the last few reels of film off to be processed. His experiment was over, and he hoped to go through the final motions as quickly as possible. He had more than enough data. There was no doubt that he could turn it into that rare creation: an interesting and readable dissertation. It would be no dry and sterile exercise. Now he looked around the room. He felt as if he had never seen the place, never lived in it, never experienced the emotions he had been through there. Everything felt unconnected to him, empty, as if he had never touched these things before, as if he were following a set of printed instructions. He watched himself, and the person he saw seemed like a stranger, like someone he had never known.

He picked the books and papers off the floor and arranged them on the desk. He swept the empty beer cans and paper cups and dust into a pile. In a short while he returned the room to the condition it was in before the raid. He could hardly remember, looking around him now, all the things that had happened there, all the weird events that had transpired between the time the colony was established and the time it ended. He stood at the desk and began to place his books back on the shelf. Something felt peculiar, but he couldn't put his finger on it. He looked for his notebooks, his data, his records of the experiment, and finally it dawned on him that they had disappeared. He thought he should feel upset, that he should feel something, but somehow it hardly mattered. He had the feeling that he could observe himself as he wandered around the room. He coldly watched himself look in places where the data might be, expecting nothing, finding what he expected. He was completely detached from his activities. He opened each drawer of the desk, drawers he had never opened before, and observed that each was still empty. He examined each trash can, moving aside the garbage and the bodies of the dead animals he had just deposited there, but again he found nothing. He went through his bookcase, volume by volume, the books that had been on the floor and those that had been untouched. He slowly walked the floor, circling the room for over an hour, feeling that he was still inside the cell. It was all a formality, an empty set of acts he was required to perform, nothing more. He was in a daze, confused, but he knew for sure that the data was gone. They would ask him if he had looked everywhere, and now he could answer that he had.

He went to the three movie cameras that were mounted on the enclosure and examined each of them in turn. He had guessed the situation in advance and felt no surprise—still felt nothing at all—when he saw that each was empty. The final films of Irving's manner of killing were gone. He went to a steel cabinet at the far end of the room, near the place where Francis had pretended to find the marijuana, and saw that all the film he had shot during the experiment was gone. There was nothing left at all. Someone had known just what they wanted. He circled the room again. It meant the end of his dissertation. There was no way of writing it without hard data. Impressionistic accounts were not accepted by the journals. His memories would not make a dissertation. He returned to the desk and looked carefully through his papers again. He looked closely at the surface and found a rectangle with less dust on it than the surrounding area. It was the place where his notebooks had been stacked. It really was all over.

Now he left the desk and returned to the enclosure. Its lights were out, and he could see himself reflected in the window. It might have looked, at first, as though he were trapped inside. He could observe himself in there with the other animals. He smiled at himself, his relaxed expression coming as no surprise. He walked up to the window and switched on the inside light. The interior was suddenly illuminated, his image gone. The place was still in good repair. With a small amount of work on the hole in the wall it could easily be readied for another colony. But he knew for certain that he would never perform another such experiment. It was impossible to imagine how he could have worked so hard and with such intensity on such a project. He could never, would never, do that again. It was a stage of life he had just passed through, and he felt no sadness at his transformation. He was finished with science, finished with all of them. The stream in him that led him to perform the experiment, that gave him his fascination and his insight, was changing course. It was going to fill his life. He was past the point of experimentation; he knew the truth about himself; it was time to live according to the things he knew.

Goldenson opened the door to the enclosure. The smell that greeted him was hardly different from the smell outside, the air cooler than it had ever felt before. He stepped inside without the revulsion he'd so often felt in the past. He could see his own reflection from the inside now, looking in on himself. It looked the same as before, as relaxed and neutral. It occurred to him that somewhere inside himself he *must* be feeling something more than this. Things couldn't be as bland or simple as they seemed. For more than a minute he looked at his reflection in the hope that he might discover what it was he felt. And then a wave of enormous sadness and fear crashed over him. There were no words for it, no way of articulating it, no way at all to think about it coherently. The pain was so great that he felt no urge to cry. He was far beyond tears. Instead he rolled onto his side, his face resting on the floor of the enclosure, and he clutched his knees against his chest and rocked himself. He became his own baby now, his own lost child, his own aborted fetus, and the walls of the enclosure were like the incubator in which he had been placed when he was born. With that idea his whole life seemed to come together; the loneliness he had always felt, the distance from all others around him. He wanted to be held now, to be lifted out of the enclosure. Maybe Wendy would come. But with another part of him he knew quite clearly he was all alone. If any lifting was to be done it would have to be with his own two hands.

He looked up from the floor. It was the animals' view of their surroundings. The walls seemed towering now, the lights in the ceiling shining down with an intensity that almost blinded him. He had known from the start that the lights were too bright but had chosen to leave them that way for the sake of the photography. Now he had the thought that the horror the rats had experienced had been his own creation. He had designed their world. He had designed his own world. They were poor dumb creatures with no opportunity to do anything except respond. He was the one who had set events in motion. All that was in it came from him, including all the horror. He was more destructive than Irving. Inside himself were a billion Irvings. He'd made them live that way, made them grow that way because he suffered in that way. Their actions were his own; extensions of himself; observing them saved him from performing them.

Now he raised himself to the level of Irving's platform. A supply of paper strips had been pressed into a makeshift nest. It was not unlike the nests of normal females. He wondered if that had been Irving's fantasy, if in some way he hoped to produce a litter of his own. The more he thought about the animal, the more he tried to fathom its experience, the more he knew that they were profoundly similar. Irving had lived out the horrors inside himself. Now they were emerging on their own, and there was no way to turn them off. They were his ideas, his fantasies, the part of him that had tormented him and yet was inaccessible to him all through his life. There was an image that flooded him now of a large, overwhelming crowd. There were dozens of bodies jammed tightly together in what might have been a series of interconnected embraces, an orgy or a struggle to the death. They were groaning, tearing at each other's clothes, tearing at each other's bodies, and he felt the whole awful weight of them press down on him.

He felt unable to control the movements of his arms and legs. Slowly, against his will, he allowed himself to slip down to the floor again. The image was overwhelming him, carrying him along with it and up into it. He knew enough about such experiences not to fight it. He could feel the weight of the bodies on his chest and legs, could smell their breath in his face. People were talking to each other, happy in the middle of the mass, and some were reading comic books and newspapers. Others were naked and copulating; others were tearing at each other's flesh. And he felt himself flow out to them and attempt to join them. When he looked up at the lights again, the bright glaring lights and the shining windows, he felt he was inside a subway car, inside a lurching evil-smelling car in the middle of a summer rush hour. He could feel all the bodies pressed against him. No longer did he recoil. Now he pressed back into them with all his might. If he could only press hard enough, if he could only push his way into them, then all would merge, without differentiation, without love or hate, without the need for any words. And he felt that he would do it. That he could manage it. That he could feel and live with them inside of him, and him inside of them. And at that moment he came.

He lay there afterward. He had gone where the flood wanted him to go. He could feel the relief come over him. He had taken the trip and now he was back. He felt alive again for the first time in many weeks. He could feel the floor and the texture of his clothes and the wet spot in his pants. He could feel his fingers when he tried to move them and the tears that filled his eyes. The image was gone. The need to subject himself to that experience was gone. The need to control it and the need to give in to it were gone. It was as if a great iceberg, around him all his life, had suddenly melted. His need to touch it, to climb it, to master it was gone as well. Finally he left the enclosure for the last time, lay down on the cot and fell into a dreamless sleep.

·27·

"I JUST KNOW," said Goldenson, "but it's impossible to explain."

Wendy looked distressed. "I believe you, but it's not enough. You have to say something more. You have to be more specific. We still need help."

"I don't want any help. I want to get out of this town." He looked her in the eye. "I want you to come with me. I really want you to be with me."

She met his gaze. "Well I'm going to see this through. I know how you feel. I know how angry you are. I know it's the worst thing he could have done to you. I'm just as angry. He's my brother, God help me. But in this situation that isn't enough. There are millions of people involved. Don't indulge yourself. Francis isn't the whole city. I have another brother, a decent one. One with possibilities. I don't want him to die. I don't want anyone else to die."

"The city is already dead. Nothing matters here anymore."

"It matters to me," Hall said. He was more angry than they had ever seen him. "There are three million black people here. They had no part in this. They get the same treatment from the police you got yourself. If you have a new insight I expect you to do something about it. You owe it to me. You owe it to all of us. I don't care what your theory is about the future of the world. I don't care if you've made peace with your own destructiveness. There's more at stake here than the state of your personality."

"Okay," said Goldenson. The remark was vague, but at least it indicated a willingness to begin. "I know, I think I know, that at some point, I don't know when, he'll go into the subway." He pointed to the enclosure. "I was in there, to clean it out, and the idea came on me. Rather, to put it more exactly, I had an experience that led me to it. I guess I had a sort of vision of the way the world is going to be, filled up with people. It was as simple as that. They were laying all over me, breathing all over me, and I hated it, and I loved it. The inside of that box became a subway car. It was something I used to do when I was a kid—ride the subway in the rush hour to feel the women pressed up against me. At least I told myself it was the women. For a while I did it every day. It's the place where Irving was born, the place inside my head where he was born. It's the place where I was born, or where I wanted to be born. And I knew—in the fantasy I knew—it was the worst experience I could imagine, it terrified me down into my balls, and also, at the same time, at exactly the same time, that I loved every second of it, that it was the most orgasmic experience that I ever had."

He looked at the others and shrugged. "Do you really expect me to tell that to the police? It's incomprehensible. I can hardly talk about it. I loved it and I hated it. That's much too mild. I adored it and I despised it. It was sex and it was beyond sex. I wanted to lose myself forever in it and I wanted to destroy it." He paused and studied them. "So on the assumption—I accept it now, I know it's the truth—that I am Irving, just as I know that the killer is also Irving, maybe a slightly different variety, but still a relative, I know what I would want to do and I know what he would want. I know that I would go into the subway. It would be, in my fantasy, the best place to go. Not only because of the logic of it, the fact that he needs a confined space because he's running out of chemicals, but also because it has a special attraction to someone like us who has a thing about huge crowds. If I felt that they were chasing me I would head there at once if I hadn't already made it home."

They looked at him. "You think because of his hang-up with crowds he would be drawn to the most crowded place that he could find?" Hall repeated his summary carefully, and glanced from Goldenson to Wendy as he talked.

"It isn't just a hang-up," Goldenson said. "It's a complicated love affair. The other side of it is the urge to lose himself. To stop existing as a separate person, to merge with the mass and become whatever it becomes. To go to Woodstock, Times Square on New Year's, a mass political rally . . . Everyone becomes one body, each one a part of everyone. A natural merger. A huge relief, at least for a while. . . . He looked into Wendy's eyes, and his expression suggested he was pleading with her to understand. "You want to become a part of them, and then you realize that if you do you don't exist. You begin to hate them. You begin to hate yourself. You end up feeling that the only hope for you is their complete destruction. But then you know, at exactly the moment that you're hoping for it, maybe planning it, that it also means the end of you. You only exist as a part of them no matter what you do. You can't escape that. . . ." Now that he had begun to talk it became important to him that they really understand. "I know it's vague. You have to think of it as a kind of trip. I'm trying to communicate a trip . . ."

Wendy touched his hand. "A bad trip. I'm glad you came back."

"I'm not completely back."

"Where are you then?" she asked.

"Someplace else. In the subway. Trying to get off the train. Trying to get away."

Hall was still looking for evidence. "Tell us specifically how you got the subway idea."

"How should I know?" Goldenson crossed the room and stood beside the enclosure. He went to the corner where Irving had dug his hole. He touched the wood the rat had chewed. The touch was like a caress. "How should I know," he repeated. "You want to get into a tunnel. You want your own place, your own territory. It's probably the reason that I let him go." He looked at Hall now. "Let me ask you something. What made you cage him in? What made you nail the water tray down? You have your own impulses. Maybe you're an Irving in reverse, a reaction-formation. Maybe you have the same thing inside of you and you're doing everything you can to keep it under control."

Hall took the comment seriously. "I won't deny that I have murder in me, something like it anyway. But it's not that general. It sure as hell doesn't apply to black people. And it only applies to certain whites. And it's not the result of crowding. It has specific historical and political origins—"

"So everyone's a killer," Wendy said. "How original. Now all we have to do is go into analysis. It's all caused by our mothers anyway." She dialed the telephone and waited as her call was routed through the department until her father came on the line.

"Dad?"

She listened as he spoke.

"Do you know about the notebooks?" she asked. "Do you know how much work they represent?" She looked at Goldenson and shook her head negatively as she listened to her father's reply. "His politics," she said into the telephone. "His self-righteous morality. His right-to-life hang-up." She listened again to her father. "Well, I hope you can do something," she said. And then, after a pause: "We have another idea. We think he might be interested in going underground, in hitting the subway ..."

She paused. "It's too complicated to explain on the telephone. We don't think he'd ever leave. We think he's here in the city and will stay until it's over—one way or the other."

Her father spoke again.

"How should I?" There was a touch of irritation in her response.

He spoke again.

She was becoming agitated. It might have been fear, or anger. "Well, isn't that stupid. How could they make such a plan? Don't they keep people in reserve?"

She listened again and became increasingly subdued. "Okay. Let's stay in touch."

She turned to Goldenson and Hall. "Dad says they're convinced he's trying to leave the city. They've decided that he needs more chemicals. They figure he'll operate on a larger and larger scale, the way he's been going. They're checking roads and trains and bus stations and airports. There's only a skeleton force on regular duty. If you want to rob a bank, fellas, now's the time."

"Only don't take the subway home," said Hall.

·28·

IT WAS, everyone was convinced, time for Irving to strike again.
Everyone in the city worried about it. When people dared to
meet in social groups it was all they talked about. Life in New
York came almost to a halt. A small percentage of city dwellers
did go about their business as if there was no terror in the air.
They were the people who always got to work on time come
snow or flood or power failure, who got a kind of righteous
pleasure out of it. Most of the others merely attempted to function. Their efforts were sporadic and inept. Life in the city was
difficult under the best of circumstances. But now, under constant threat, it was near impossible. Even the most insignificant
act became a major challenge and strain. A trip to the corner
market for a container of milk was now a foray into potentially
murderous territory. It was no longer just a fear of muggers—
the old terror was trivial beside the new one. Street crime, in
fact, almost disappeared. There were fewer policemen on the
streets, but it seemed, along with everyone else, the muggers
were at home and watching television.

And if one did go out and then return alive to one's apartment, perhaps clutching a container of milk or a six-pack of
beer, the terror was far from over. One could never be certain
that one's food or drink had not been poisoned. Several deaths
from poisoned produce had already been reported. Whether
they were caused by the killer or by others adopting his method
to their own purpose was not clear. One tried to purchase

things in cans—the older the better. But whatever the form in which one's food arrived, it was a source of worry. One was left contemplating it, perhaps sniffing it tentatively, but then, sooner or later, unless one tried it first on the dog or cat, one was forced to take the plunge. Digestion under such conditions was hardly a pleasure; one counted oneself lucky if one didn't fall to the floor in a convulsing heap.

One waited. One monitored one's body to make certain there were no early signs. One never knew what to expect with enough clarity to rule out any peculiar feeling. One consulted one's doctor as often as possible only to find, a good deal of the time, that he had moved his practice. If one really needed to be seen he would be happy to oblige if one traveled to the suburb in which he lived. The use of everything from heroin to thorazine, from valium to alcohol increased dramatically. A rumor spread through the city that alcohol was an antidote to parathion. Like most such myths, the opposite was the truth, but it persisted despite repeated television discussions and denials.

Television became the center. It was the way people connected. But it was even more unreal than before. Most of the programs discussing the situation featured people who would never enter the city. The programs came from Chicago or Washington or Los Angeles. And though there were some expressions of real concern, a feeling of contempt began to show itself, an implication that New York deserved what it was getting. It was the fiscal crisis all over again, although considerably more grotesque. A prominent southwestern senator was quoted as having said at a cocktail party that the killer was doing the rest of the country a favor. Despite a proper storm of protest, he made no retraction or apology.

One controversy after another raged. There was something new to contemplate each day. The tube glowed. But at best it was all distraction. Beneath the unending words, beneath the vacant pronouncements, the people of New York City knew the truth: there was someone out to kill as many of them as possible and he was still able to do it with impunity.

·29·

THEY MET THE Black Angels in Goldenson's laboratory. The
first eleven came early, one by one, which was fine with Wendy
and Goldenson—each that appeared looked more menacing
than the one before. They were dressed well, in bright and
sometimes expensive clothing, and they laughed and joked
among themselves, but their expressions implied they had already lived a lifetime, and their scars implied that perhaps one
lifetime was enough. They had all been addicts. Each had been
on his own for years, had survived the life of the streets. All had
been in serious trouble. All were still angry. They were young
people who could enter a subway car alone, at any time of the
day or night, and with one look frighten everyone, no matter what their race or politics. In a group they could frighten
themselves.

"Where is he?" Hall paced the floor. He looked at his watch
again and again and stared at the others.

Finally the latecomer arrived. He was out of breath and his
pale green silk shirt was stained with sweat. "I'm sorry man,"
he began to explain. "There's this dude—"

"Forget it," said Hall. "I don't want to know about it. If it
happens again you're out of it. Same for anyone else. What you
have to remember ..." he looked significantly at the two
whites. ... "What we all have to remember, is that if we go
ahead with this, we all depend on each other. Our *lives* depend
on it. All our lives. We have to take care of each other. Either

we do it right or I'll stay out of it." He stood in the middle of the room and pulled himself up to his full six-four.

To Wendy and Goldenson, Hall appeared transformed. It was a side of him he'd never shown them before. They knew he worked with this gang but they'd been under the impression that he functioned more as a social worker. Here he was coming on like a parent.

"Come on man, you know we take care," another youngster said. It was Simba, the leader of the group.

"I know it," Hall said more softly, "but my friends don't. I told them I trust you, but that doesn't mean they will. We function on real time here, not Colored People's Time."

"Okay, man. The cat fucked up. We get your message. Don't make too much of it. We know we trust each other. We all are in it. We've been hurt by this bastard just like everybody else."

Hall nodded. He turned to Wendy and Goldenson. "Three people in this room have relatives that got a dose of poison. One of us"—he looked at a silent youngster—"ate some of that rice himself. We've all had enough."

Simba spoke up again. "The question of trust comes back to you." He looked at Wendy and Goldenson. "I don't mean trust you to protect our asses. We can handle that. We were doing it before your buddy came to work with us." He was obviously intelligent, and he spoke as clearly and precisely as Hall had. "What I mean, what we all mean, is trust your purposes. If we're going to put our asses on the line, then it has to make sense. It has to be mean-ing-ful." He looked at Hall and smiled. "One thing we learned from our big brother here is to use our brains. We're thinking motherfuckers now. We don't just jump when the feeling comes on us. We don't just burn some dude cause we're in the mood."

Goldenson had been warned by Hall that he would be questioned closely, so now he described his experiment in detail, making sure that they understood, taking great pains not to talk down to them. He showed them the enclosure and pointed out the perch that Irving had used. He showed them the hole the animal had made and the place in the floor where he had found his freedom. He tried to explain the connection between the killer and Irving. He was aware, as he talked, that a major part of it, his own inner experience, was missing, but he had no intention of going into that. It was the way he'd felt when talking to the police: he could describe the parallels, but the part that explained his insights had to be left out.

Simba quickly grasped the heart of the problem. "Why the subway?" he asked. "Why don't he use some basement somewhere? Why not the sewers?"

"That's another place trust comes in," said Wendy. It was a conscious attempt to rescue Goldenson. "That's where we trust him," nodding toward Goldenson. They all turned to her, and several looked at her body in a way that made their thoughts very clear. "He has a feeling for this thing. It's worked so far. He's been right all along. I know I trust his feeling. I know Ed Hall trusts it. Even the police are beginning to trust it, or at least they say they do. They think we may be right, but they won't commit the men to it. It's too much of a long shot. They say they have to play the probabilities. They would accept our plan. We'd get their okay. But they'd only help us if we found something. They'd let us do it our way, but we'd have to do it on our own."

A huge, muscular boy smiled at her. His eyes were half closed. "Baby, you and me could do something on our own—"

"If you pull that shit we might as well forget it." She stared hard at him when she said it.

"Cool it, Jumbo," the leader said. "And if we do find something, if we take the chance and nail the mother, and then the police come in, say at the very end, what happens then?"

"I don't follow you," she said.

"Like the credit, baby. Like the *reward*." One hundred thousand dollars reward had been offered by a group of banks and department stores.

"We split that," said Hall. "The way I told you. Half goes to us and the other half you divide. If all twelve are in it would be over four thousand each. You don't have to worry about the police. They're not eligible. It's their job—"

"I know better than that. There's rip-offs every day."

"He's right. You can't trust the police." It was the smallest member of the group, a boy they all called Yo-Yo. "There's no fuckin' way you can trust the police. They got relatives, man, they pull all kinds of shit." He stepped up close to Goldenson and pulled his sleeve up to reveal a scarred and twisted arm. "You see what they did to me."

"We all have our problems," Hall said. "We've all been kicked in the balls."

"Not all of us," Jumbo said, looking at Wendy again.

"Some are going to get it a second time," she said.

The boys all laughed, Yo-Yo the loudest, until Jumbo threatened him with his huge fist.

"There's too much publicity," Hall went on. "There's no way they could do us out of it."

"Don't be so sure," another boy said. "Yo-Yo's right. They pull a relative out of the hat. They claim, after it's over, that he supplied the information. They come up with all kinds of bullshit. They give you fifty dollars and tell you to go fuck off."

"We already have a relative," Wendy said. They turned to her again. "It's me. My father's on the force. We've already worked with him. He's been helpful to us and he's done what we asked of him. You don't have to worry about the money. What you do have to worry about is whether we'll catch the bastard who's pulling all this stuff, and what we'll do with him if we do get hold of him, or what he'll do to us."

"You leave that to me," Jumbo said.

"I don't work with no police," another boy said. He was thin and handsome, dressed simply and elegantly, and was known by the name of Bullet for the .22-caliber slug still lodged in his skull. "I don't want any part of it." He began to get up, and it looked as if there were several who were preparing to leave with him.

"You're not the only victims around here," Goldenson said. "Don't make it into such a big deal." They stood and looked at him, and for a moment it seemed there might be violence. "They locked me up. They harassed me. They ripped off all my notes. I've been working on this experiment for a year and three of them just wiped out all my records. I'd say I'm entitled to as much hatred as any of you. But that's beside the point now. We're not in this for the police, or with the police. Getting Irving is our personal *private* operation. We'll get what we can from them, but we'll do it on our *own*. We don't *want* their help. We just want them to let us alone, let us do it the way we plan to. They're so desperate they'll go along. They have to go along."

Bullet and Simba looked at each other. "We want to talk about it," Simba said. "You folks just go for a little walk." Wendy and Goldenson started for the door. "All you folks," he said to Hall.

The three of them left the basement and strolled around the campus. There was little for them to talk about. Each was involved with private consequences. For Hall it was a test of his relationship with the group. If they backed off now it was hard to see how he could go on working with them. For Goldenson it was his first real chance of getting at the killer, at the Irving at loose outside. He could never have worked closely with the police. Now he might be directly involved in the action, now he might test his idea. And if they found the killer ... well, it would be his last and best experiment. Validated.

In fifteen minutes they returned to the laboratory.

"Write it down," Simba said. "We're in it, but we want a contract. We want you to spell it out on paper."

"Right," said Goldenson, his excitement building. He extended his hand and the other shook it. Then he sat down at the typewriter.

·30·

WENDY TOOK THE BUS to the Bronx. A cab would be too expensive she felt, and the subway was of course out of the question. She had to transfer three times and it took her two hours. She didn't call in advance, just went with the knowledge that James was at school and the others at work. She let herself in with the key she had not had to use in years. The place was neat, as usual, but smelled peculiar. Smelled too much, she thought, of men. She was amused to find herself thinking that way. No sooner did she get into the vicinity of her family than she found herself feeling domestic. It was another of the reasons she preferred to stay away. She walked silently through the first floor of the house. She knew that the odds were against her but she couldn't allow Francis to get away with what he had done. She assumed he would hide Goldenson's data in a place where neither their father nor James would come across it—she was certain they would never go along with him in such a vicious act. She worked carefully and methodically, resisting the impulse to dust or straighten as she searched each of the rooms. She found nothing on the first floor. It was the least likely place, and she thought he might hide it there for that reason. But she should have known he had no capacity to be subtle. She would have to try the basement and the upstairs rooms.

The door to the basement was in the kitchen, and as she opened it, along with the damp smell, a memory of her childhood rushed up at her. There had been a time when she was terrified of that place. Once there had been an old furnace there. It was the job of the boys to keep it stoked with coal, but sometimes she had to go down into the basement on an errand of some sort, even times when she was alone in the house and had to go feed the furnace herself. There had always been a fear of that squat dark creature there, a beast of her own, with glowing red eyes that could only be seen when the lights were out and a huge mouth, swallowing lumps of black stone, a poor substitute for what she was sure it really wanted: her life.

And Francis had always known about her fear. One time in the middle of the winter when it had to be stoked regularly he had pretended to go out to play and instead came back in through the basement door and waited behind the furnace for her to appear. He growled and moaned as she stood with the shovel in her hand and she froze and peed in her pants. She had flung the coal and shovel at him when he laughed at her afterward, but the humiliation was still there, would probably always be there.

Now the basement had been modernized. There was an oil burner in its own compartment. The walls had been paneled with knotty pine, the floor tiled, and there was a chrome and plastic bar. On one wall was a row of unused fish tanks, an old hobby of James', containing nothing now but a layer of dry gravel, and beside them a row of rifles, Francis' hobby, in a locked case. The room seemed hardly used. They had set it up in the hope of developing something like a family life, but none had come along. Now it was a place where Francis sometimes drank with his hunting buddies and showed his rifles off. There was nothing else there, so she decided to go upstairs to examine the bedrooms.

She climbed the creaky stairs to the second floor and briefly examined James' and her father's rooms. She felt reasonably certain that Francis wouldn't have had the nerve to hide anything there. She went down to the end of the hall to the room Francis now occupied. It was the room she had slept in when she lived with them and the boys had had to share. She always had a fond memory of it, one of the few fond memories of that house, and she paused for a moment at the window and peered out into the small backyard with the huge maple tree, where once she had her own swing. She turned back to the room and looked around. The bed was unmade, and on the floor beside it was an empty beer can, an overflowing ashtray, and a stack of magazines. Their lurid contents were no great surprise to her as she glanced at them. She replaced them and at the same time peered under the bed in the hope of discovering the missing data and film. But all that she found was dust. She examined his closet, his bookshelves on which there were only more magazines, and even the pile of dirty laundry in one corner of the room.

She decided to reexamine the basement—it still seemed the most likely possibility. She again went down the stairs and methodically searched the room. In a storage closet she came across a scrapbook of photographs she'd made in her teen-age years, and in a suitcase of clothes she found her first bra. God! She remembered the embarrassment her breasts had caused her then. She remembered how Francis always looked at her. But there was still no sign of the data, and she was not there on a nostalgia trip. Finally she stood motionless in the middle of the room, turned slowly and tried to concentrate. Maybe like Goldenson she could use her intuition. She would use her body as a dousing rod. But it wasn't her body or her intuition that gave her the clue—it was her memory. She noticed that the gravel in the fish tanks was deeper than when they had held living fish. She put her hand into a tank . . . and felt an envelope. She pulled it out, spilling gravel onto the floor, opened it, and saw at once that it was a portion of Goldenson's data.

Now she systematically examined each tank. And in each, carefully placed within a sealed envelope, she found more of the missing data. She brushed the gravel away and piled each package in the middle of the room. The film was there as well. The last tank yielded an envelope of a different shape and texture from the others. Inside were guarantee cards and a set of instructions for a portable spray gun. Peculiar—

"Get away from there."

She turned slowly, the picture of the spray gun still in her hand. It was Francis, and he held a police revolver. "My God, Francis, you must be completely crazy to—"

"And you're a goddamn snooping bitch."

"You know," she said, "I believe you're actually capable of killing me."

He returned the gun to his holster. "Not yet, but I'm getting there."

"How could you do this?" she asked. "Don't you have any decency? He worked his guts out on this for over a year. He never did anything to you."

"Believe me, it's nothing personal. As far as I'm concerned he's a hippie creep just like a couple of hundred thousand others."

"So why bother? He could file a complaint against you. I'd testify."

"I'll bet you would. Okay I have two reasons," Francis said. "I hate his bullshit research. He has no right to do what he does to innocent animals and he has no right to do what he plans to do with his results."

"Meaning what?"

"I'm not so dumb, you know. I know what these population creeps are looking for."

"What the hell are you talking about?"

"He's going to use his phony findings to help the abortionists. He'll give them a phony picture of what the world is coming to, of what he wants people to believe it's coming to, and then they'll use it to make propaganda for abortions. I've read his letters. I know who's interested. I know who's offered him a grant."

"Are you still into that? Why don't you worry about your own sins? You must spend plenty of time jerking off over those magazines upstairs."

He grew calm, and cold. "There are sins and sins. They're not all the same."

"You worry about yours and I'll worry about mine."

"I'm not worried about yours. I've given up on you, but I haven't given up on your younger brother."

"You figure hurting Goldenson and me helps James? The logic is brilliant. It's as good as your abortion theory. What are you really driving at?"

"Well, use your famous intelligence," he said. "I was going to offer you a deal, I *am* offering you a deal."

She tried to lift the folders off the floor, but found that the pile was too ungainly. She went up to the kitchen for some string and when she got back she saw that he'd taken the envelope with the spray gun instructions. "And what the hell is *that* about?" she asked.

"My own experiment, none of your business." He watched her tie Goldenson's data into a manageable package. "I'm still offering you a deal," he finally said. "Stay away from James. Just keep your distance. Stop trying to influence him. I'm warning you. I'll keep away from you and your boyfriend. If you don't listen to me something dangerous is going to happen—"

"Something dangerous is happening anyway," she said. "Remember?" She lifted the package now and left the house by the basement door. In the street she would hail a cab.

·31·

HALL HAD CHOSEN a candy store a few blocks from the college as their base of operations. They sat there now, all three of them, on a street too dangerous for them as whites to have visited before, in a small dirty store, sipping second cups of coffee. Outside, directly in front of the window, a numbers runner took bets, and across the street, barely concealed in the doorway of an abandoned building, a pusher dispensed bags of heroin to his frequent customers.

"Someday we get that mother," the youngster—his name was Willie—standing beside them said.

"No one in the Angels is on drugs anymore," Hall said. "The group makes sure of that. That in itself makes it worthwhile, no matter what trouble they get into."

The youngster slid into the booth. Without being asked, the man behind the counter brought him coffee. He filled his cup with plenty of milk and three heaping spoons of sugar, then sipped with obvious pleasure.

"Where are they at?" Goldenson asked.

The boy looked first at Hall and then at Goldenson. "Nowhere," he replied. "Just getting into it nice and slow. Just checking out the scene, getting the feel of it."

"Where have you been?" Hall asked. He extracted a small pad from his pocket and made notes as the boy talked.

"I been on the A train," he said. "I walked the tracks from

One-twenty-fifth to One-forty-fifth. I took my time. We're all takin' our time. I didn't see anything."

"We've assigned someone to every track that crosses Harlem," Hall explained. "We'll check our own turf first and then worry about the rest of the city. These dudes all know their way around. They've played around down there for years. They used to write their names on trains."

The youngster beamed. He looked younger than his fifteen years. "I saw one of my own," he said. "I can't believe it. I'm dragging my ass along there on the express track and this local goes by, slowing up for a station, and I look and see my own name floating by. It's two years since I put it there. I can even remember the night I did it. I did one whole car. I figure it's a sign," he went on. "A good omen. We're gonna find the mother and pick up on that cash."

They sat there and smiled at each other, each feeling a sense of adventure and enjoying it. At least in a small way, the whites had apparently been accepted.

When he finished his coffee Willie checked his digital watch, then nodded and left the store. Soon another youngster arrived, he took his seat and casually accepted his coffee as Hall extracted the notebook once again.

"Broadway–Seventh Avenue Line," the boy said. "One-sixteenth to One-thirty-seventh. The uptown local tracks. No sign of anything." His information was precise. "I talked to Little J., the cat on the downtown track, and he ain't seen nothin' either."

"Is it hard to find your way around?" Wendy asked.

"No sweat. I done it years ago. One time my ma's old man was out to get me and I hid down there a week. That time I had no flashlight."

"You're looking for side places?" Hall asked. "Tunnels? Places where he might bed down?"

"We're looking everywhere," the youngster said emphatically. "We like the action and we like the cash. We're havin' a fine old time." He checked his watch—another digital—drained his coffee and left with a wave.

"How long do you think it'll last?" Wendy asked.

They looked at her, surprised.

"It's too good to be true," she went on. "It isn't all going to be a picnic. You don't expect them to come up with something the first day. There's more than a hundred miles to cover. It's going to get a little boring after a while."

"You sound like my old teacher," said Hall. "The year they left me back. You underestimate these kids. Everyone claims they have a short attention span, but if you put them into something that interests them I can assure you that they have no problem."

She nodded silently and remembered that in his youth Hall had had problems not so different from the kind the gang was living through. He too had spent his time in reform school.

Now they sat there quietly. There was little to say. Each felt jumpy, partly from the coffee but mostly from the situation. It was the beginning of something that had a feel of randomness about it yet each felt in his or her own way a kind of certainty. They were more sophisticated than the kids, less awed by the money, less certain that things would turn out well, yet each in his own way felt the same excitement.

Finally Hall checked his watch. "They should all be back by now. Let's see what the story is."

They left the candy store and walked through the dirty streets. It was evening now, but the community somehow seemed less ominous than it had before. Children played in front of houses. Men and women returned from work. Many smiled at Hall, who was obviously well known in the neighborhood. They turned a corner and went down a flight of stairs to a basement door. Key in hand, Hall opened it quickly and stepped in before them. They entered a short hallway and then a large, pleasantly furnished room with couches and chairs and a folding table in the center.

"Welcome," Yo-Yo said. He bowed deeply in front of Wendy. He seemed to be the one to play the role of clown.

"Pleased to be here," she replied, and curtsied.

Hall glanced around the room. Everyone was there. On time. In the center, underneath the table, was a pile of green plastic garbage bags. Each was carefully tied and labeled. On top of the table was a New York City subway map. The lines that crossed through Harlem were circled in red, and beside each circle, also in red, a name was written.

"Any problems?" Hall asked. "Anything unusual?"

His questions were met with silence. "I just wish I had brought some paint," said Yo-Yo. "I could have done me a train."

"Let's get into it." Hall consulted his notebook. "Let's start with the east side, the Lexington Avenue Line."

The boys extracted four plastic bags from under the table. One spread newspaper on the linoleum, another rolled a trash can into the room. Bullet untied a plastic bag and dumped his load onto the floor. "Plain old subway shit," he said. They all watched carefully as he lifted the trash, piece by piece, and dropped it into the can. There were scraps of paper, plastic coffee cups, candy wrappers, a bag with the name of a department store, and an empty wallet. "Some mother got ripped off," he said. It all was covered with a film of dirt and looked as if it had been on the tracks for years.

"We'll have the cleanest subway in the world," said Hall.

"Not for long," Bullet said.

The next youngster emptied his bag. Its contents were about the same as the first. "More crap," he said. Then, deadpan, he reached into the pile and extracted a dried condom.

The remaining trash was less interesting: newspapers, paper bags of moldy food, occasional theater ticket stubs and losing lottery tickets—the standard detritus of life in the city. But finally in a bag from the Broadway line, something caught their eyes—two pieces of cardboard, cleaner than most of what they'd found and obviously not long on the tracks, with the word "portable" on one piece and "spray gun" on the other. The youngster who found them held them beside each other, and it was obvious that they fit together. They had been torn from the same container.

"We got the mother," someone said after a moment of shocked silence.

The boy who'd found the scraps extended his palm and the others slapped it.

Simba approached Goldenson with his hand extended. "I thought you were a little nuts," he said. "I don't anymore."

Goldenson took the hand, surprised at the speed of the discovery. He found that he was frightened. "Incredible," was all he could say.

"Shit." Wendy was looking at the scraps of cardboard. "I don't believe this."

The congratulations ceased abruptly. Everyone turned to her. Her hand was shaking as she held the cardboard.

"What the hell's happening?" Hall asked.

"I've seen this before," Wendy announced.

They all looked at her, thoroughly confused.

"I have to see my father," she said to Goldenson. She took his hand and pulled him toward the door.

•32•

WENDY AND GOLDENSON took a cab downtown. They would meet the gang in the morning. She had promised to explain. Meanwhile they would prepare to search the tunnel. "It's a false alarm," she said quietly to Goldenson.

"What are you talking about?"

"I saw that carton when I found your data and film. Francis is up to something. I knew he wouldn't just leave us alone."

Goldenson was stunned. "Do you think *he's* involved in the killing?"

She looked at him seriously. "One Irving is enough. I could be wrong, God knows what he's capable of, but mostly I think he's just trying to confuse us. I think he's so crazy angry at me he doesn't care about the consequences. No matter what. He's still trying to keep me away from my little brother. I think he's ready to do anything to screw us up. He wants me to look stupid, it's always been a big thing with him. He wants to discredit me and you too, anybody I'm involved with. That's what he's really got against you—me. I don't think he cares a damn about the danger."

Goldenson sat silently as the cab sped along. He had no idea what to say, but finally it occurred to him that words were unnecessary. Unwise, in fact. He put his arm around her and she put her head against his chest and began to cry. It was the first time she'd showed her pain and the first time he felt really able to comfort her. It felt strange, but very right. "It's really crazy," he said finally. "As if the real danger isn't bad enough."

Her crying stopped. Her mind began to work again. "All he had to do was take the subway," she said. "He could stand between the cars and drop stuff onto the tracks. It would have been easy enough for him to find out what we were up to. The police know all about us. We know some of them are keeping an eye on us."

"The kids are right," Goldenson said. "We can't trust anyone. We really do have to do it on our own. . . ."

They entered police headquarters and went directly to her father's office. They were told he was in a meeting, and waited numbly until he finished. His expression was grim when he appeared, and he looked worn out. They suspected they must look about the same. She brought her father up to date, her tears coming again as she told the story of her confrontation with her brother.

He took the news calmly. It was obvious that he thought her conclusions about Francis were correct. "He's gone too far," he said finally. "I told him to control himself. That last deal he pulled was more than enough," he said with a look at Goldenson.

"You knew he was up to something?" she asked.

"I know the way he feels about James, where he should go to school, his life. I know his anger toward the two of you. I know how irrational he's gotten to be."

He let them sit there, the tears still streaking his daughter's face. It was apparent that the situation contained great bitterness and pain for him. He had to weigh concern for his daughter and her rather wayward life on one hand, for his eldest son on the other, and for the future of his youngest son on yet a third. He was struggling with things that went back many years, and he was still conscious of the debt he owed his daughter. Finally he spoke: "James is going to the University of Chicago. You win. He told us last night, and Francis was enraged. He said he still had time to prove to James that you and your ideas were worthless. He stormed out of the house. I thought he was going to see his girl friend."

She started to cry again, then reached out to her father

and wrapped her hand around his. "It's not so bad, it's still a family ..."

"Almost," he said. "Almost. It's Francis now who's killing that."

"You have to stop him," she said. "It's dangerous. One false alarm won't stop us, but God knows what else he might try."

Her father looked increasingly upset. "I called his girl's house this morning. He never got there. He never got to work either. I thought he was walking the streets somewhere, or holed up in some bar—"

"He's apparently got other diversions," Goldenson said.

"He won't hurt you," McGhie said. "I know him. He never would hurt you."

"He'll hurt what we're doing," Goldenson said. "He has already. That's bad enough."

"These kids are really doing something?" McGhie said. "They really care about this thing? We know they're a bunch of hoods. They're muggers and worse. Every one of them has a record—"

"You can't tell the good guys so easily anymore," Goldenson said. "Everything's reversed ..." He cut off his bitterness when he saw the pain in both their faces. "They're trying," he went on. "They're serious. They're very much involved in the hunt, and of course the reward. We're *all*, in our fashion, trying."

McGhie studied the two of them. Hell, maybe in this crazy deal they really were the only hope—his daughter, her professor boyfriend, and, God help him, a bunch of ghetto kids with records long as your arm. Shaking his head, he got to his feet and motioned them to wait as he left the room. Soon he returned with a stack of leaflets. "We decided to go ahead with these," he said. "That's what my meeting was about. There was still a lot of opposition," he said to Goldenson. "You know the complications, but we've decided it's time to take the risk. Our people have been using them at the roadblocks and sooner or later it's bound to get around. His family is being notified right now. The press is holding off, but in two days it'll be in the papers and all over television. You might as well take some. Maybe you can use them now. If you nail someone, it might as well be the right person. Just make sure it doesn't get around."

He handed each of them a leaflet. It was an enlarged repro-

152

duction of the killer's photograph, the one he'd already shown to Goldenson. The bland expression was the same, as well as the absence of unique features. The skin was smooth and unlined. It looked like a man who had never experienced the things in life that eventually mark a person's face. Indeed, it looked like a man who had hardly experienced anything.

Goldenson again stared intently at the picture.

"I assume you're sure," Wendy said. There was something about the face that made her turn away.

"Absolutely," said her father. "We wouldn't distribute this casually. We had to go slow. We had to be certain. We finally deciphered a fingerprint on one of the sprayers he used downtown. The middle finger on his right hand. It's locked up tight."

"But you haven't anything more on where he is?" Goldenson asked.

"Nothing."

They got ready to leave. "We'll let you know, of course, if anything . . . happens," Wendy said.

"Yes, well, I want to hear from you, but we have our own sources too. We're not quite as out of it as some people think." He looked at Goldenson. "I hope you're going to be careful," he said. "Both of you."

"We've been on the outside," Wendy said. "Tomorrow we go into the tunnel." She thought she saw him about to protest and added, "We're going to do it, dad. Unless you lock us all up."

He nodded. "Just watch yourselves," he said and got to his feet. He embraced Wendy and shook Goldenson's hand. "Don't worry about your brother. I'll put an alarm out on him. I'll find him and I *will* lock *him* up. Let me get a car to take you back uptown."

·33·

THEY LEFT THE POLICE CAR at the college gate. His laboratory, they felt, was still the safest and most convenient place to rest. The college looked eerie in the dark. The last of the evening classes was over and the campus was almost deserted. The buildings were still lighted, the warm classroom lights shining inside and the brighter silver lights on the massive stone surfaces outside. There was a strange beauty about the place. Though there was no ivy on the walls, though the school had more than its share of political and financial crisis, more than its share of inept professors, something powerful and moving did manage to fill its atmosphere and affect its students. Wendy recalled, as they crossed the quadrangle, that the buildings had been carved from the very heart of New York City—they were, in fact, made of stone that had been excavated in the construction of the subways.

They entered the science building, went down the flights of stairs, and Goldenson unlocked his heavy door. Everything had been dusted, washed, polished, and seemed so unfamiliar that they felt, for a moment, that it was the wrong place. Or perhaps they had already changed so much that their memory of it was altered. But the enclosure was still there, looking ominous now, as well as the cot where so often before they had made love. He locked the door behind them and switched some music on. There would be no problem with the custodial staff, or with the night watchman—everyone was accustomed to his unusual hours. There was nothing to do but rest until the appointed time, eight hours away, and as a final acknowledgment of his commitment, he set the alarm clock. She opened the refrigerator and fished out the single remaining can of beer.

They sat together on the cot in semi-darkness and took turns sipping the beer. Though when they'd left her father both had felt completely exhausted, they now found that they had no desire at all to sleep. There was just the steady buildup of tension over things to come. The fact that the room had been cleaned, that it no longer contained the smells, the aura of the animals that once had been the reason for their coming there made the experience of waiting more strained than it had ever been in the past. A part of their lives was rapidly fading, and they were painfully conscious of its passing and of the loss of the special intimacy they'd shared during those long hours of the experiment. It was in this antiseptic room that they had glimpsed a perspective on the future, and felt an excitement, and a dread as well. Now, perhaps on the verge of confronting it, they could do little more than sit and sip the last of the delicious beer.

Goldenson put his arm around Wendy's shoulder, and she placed an arm around his waist. She opened the buttons of his shirt and kissed his chest and neck. It was obvious now that she wanted to make love, and he cradled her head in his hand as she kissed his body with increasing passion. Finally, reluctantly, he told her, "I can't do it."

She was not at all upset. Her movements became less passionate, more mothering. Their positions reversed. Soon she was sitting upright and his head was in her lap. She stroked his hair and kissed his ear. He lay there, taking no initiative of his own, as if in a pool of water that was lifting him, carrying him, keeping him warm. "Are you nervous?" She assumed he was thinking about tomorrow's meeting.

"The opposite," he said. "I'm just plain drained."

"Are you afraid?"

"Yes." His voice was hollow, and she had the image of him speaking to her from the bottom of a deep pit. "Not of him. Of myself."

"Of what about yourself?"

"Everything," he said.

"I don't understand."

His eyes remained closed tight.

"Really, maybe you should try to get it all out. Maybe you could get over it."

"I don't want to get it all out," he said.

"Just talk. Say anything."

"I can't. You don't realize what you're asking—"

"I know more than you think I know." She held him for a long time. Finally he turned his face against her breasts. At first she thought he was sexually aroused, but just as he seemed to be coming out of his strange mood the full force of his feeling broke over him. As he shuddered, she rocked him against her breasts. She knew there was nothing for her to say. The important thing was that she ride it out with him. She had glimpsed his insides, and she knew the only thing for her to do was be with him. The fact that he could share his feeling with her was enough—tolerate her being there, not have to hide, allow her to hold him. It was a kind of growth, for both of them.

She held him there, just resting herself, wondering what it would be like to nurse his baby, thinking about a life together, until the alarm went off and he woke up. She could tell right away that he was feeling better. He kissed her breasts with passion, and now she could feel that he was truly ready to make love. Except that now there was no time.

They walked through the empty streets to the meeting place, and he told her about his dream. It was an image of the two of them on a small farm in the mountains, just the two of them with animals, and with corn and other vegetables growing in the sun. Down the road—a long way down the road—there might be other people, other farms, people who felt the way they did about life and about the land, perhaps a place to swim and fish, and woods and mountains in which to walk and hunt for mushrooms. He had seen the two of them there, seen them clearly, felt with every single cell inside him how beautiful a life like that would be.

"I would go with you," she said quietly. "I would go today. I would go right *now*."

"Tomorrow," he said. "We have things to do. We have to think about it."

"I've thought about it. I thought about it while you were asleep."

He smiled and put his arm around her. "Well I have to think about it. I meant it, I mean it, but I have to think more about it. I have to live with it a little while. Besides, there are complications, things we'd have to work out in advance—"

"Such as?"

"Children."

"Meaning what?"

"I don't want to make an Irving."

She squeezed his shoulder as they turned the corner and Ed Hall, in front of the candy store, came into view.

"Irving was made by his environment," she said. "Outside of the city, up in the mountains, there would be no chance of that."

·34·

FROM HIS BOOTH in the candy store Hall saw them coming. He stepped outside and met them in the street. He extended his arms and all three of them embraced. It was as if he felt the glow between Wendy and Goldenson and wanted to be part of it, and they were willing to share it with him. They walked, arms linked, around the corner toward the clubhouse. "We're ready," he said, and turned to Wendy. "So tell me what's going on, what got you so upset."

"It's her brother," Goldenson did the talking. "He's trying to louse things up." He held her hand as he went on. "She saw the box that cardboard came from in his house. She thinks he put it on the track to screw us up."

"I don't know what to think," she interrupted. "I don't know what the hell to think. Last night I thought it was a crazy trick. Then we saw my father and heard about my brother and now I'm more confused. Maybe it isn't a trick. Maybe it's real. I mean, maybe he's freaked out, maybe he's decided to follow Irving's example."

"So we still don't know what's happening," said Hall. "Not that that state of affairs is particularly new." He thought quickly and made his own decision. "We're either after your brother or the original Irving, or both. If it is your brother, either he's doing a diversionary number or something a lot more serious, which I gather he's more than capable of. I don't see that we have any choice, or rather any favorite target. We're here, and

158

we're ready, and we have to see what we can find. If it's a trick, it's a trick. The worst that can happen is that we get some practice for a confrontation later."

They went into the clubhouse. All the gang members were waiting. Most had spent the night there; many had not slept at all. Flashlights were laid out in a neat row on the table. Yo-Yo displayed a large cardboard carton. "The police brought a present," he said, with the wonder of it still in his voice. "The first one *they* ever gave me. It came an hour ago. A cop knocked on the door, polite as anything, and handed it to us. He left this note." There was an envelope addressed to Wendy.

The carton was filled with brown canvas shoulder bags. Each contained a gas mask. "It's the equipment they use themselves," said Wendy. "My father must have gotten hold of it." She opened the note and saw that it was from her father.

"Fantastic!"

Each of them selected a canvas bag and tried on a mask. It was old military surplus equipment, probably less than fully effective but it might give them a little extra time if they were sprayed with poison. The masks probably gave them, Wendy thought, a false sense of security. Now they looked like weird insects with huge plastic eyes that reflected the images of each other as they walked around the room and stared into each other's faces. There were also masks for Wendy and Goldenson, who tried them on, and now they all were indistinguishable—a swarm of bugs that someone, somewhere, was waiting to destroy. They meant to sting him first, if they could only find him.

At a signal from Hall they removed their masks and returned them to the canvas bags. Each took a flashlight from the table and inserted it into the bag beside the mask. "What does your father say?" Hall asked Wendy as Wendy folded the note.

"He tells me to be careful," she said. "He tells me my brother's still on the loose and wishes us all good luck." She held out the letter for him to see.

Hall made no attempt to take it. He looked at her, nodded. "Ready to roll?"

"Weapons," Bullet said quickly. It had obviously been on his mind.

"We promised not to carry," Yo-Yo said. As usual, he smiled.

"We can't go naked," Goldenson said, surprising himself.

They all turned to him. It was confirmation he was with them. As if he'd been given a signal, Bullet now left the room. He returned with a small, heavy carton. Opening it, he revealed a pile of new, glistening, black and chrome switchblade knives. "We stick the fucker," he said quietly.

They gathered around the table and each selected a knife.

"Feels like the old days," Jumbo said. "We go find some fat honkie to take off."

Hall gave him a serious look.

"I only spoofin', bro," he said to Goldenson. "Our big bro reformed us. We the good guys now."

They were ready. The teasing abruptly halted. They gathered around the table for their final instructions.

"Wait," said Goldenson, and reached into his pocket. "I almost forgot." He passed the photograph to each of them. "Irving has been identified—if you do have to stick someone, here's the man. They're sure he's the one. They're sure he works alone. It seems a lot of our guesses turned out to be correct."

"Big Irving," Yo-Yo said, studying the picture. "You just another honkie."

The boy who had eaten the poisoned rice stared silently into the man's blank eyes. His lips were moving, but no one could make out what he was saying.

Bullet was also silent. He snapped his finger against the corner of the page.

Hall looked up from the photograph and at Goldenson. He was clearly annoyed. "You almost *forgot*? What the hell goes on? Are you letting him down the drain again? We don't have just this bastard to contend with, we have her brother. And now we have you."

Goldenson shrugged in embarrassment. He was unable to explain himself.

Now it was Wendy's turn to protect him. "The police aren't releasing it for another two days. They don't want copies to get out prematurely." Like Hall, she studied Goldenson. Was there, she wondered, another reason he had forgotten? Was it anything more than the pressure of the last few days?

"This photo won't help anyway," Yo-Yo said. They turned to him. "White folks all look alike."

Everybody laughed, including Hall, and Bullet slapped Yo-Yo's turned-up palm.

"Okay, let's get it on," said Hall. He looked at his watch. "It's time for A group to move." Five of the boys started for the door. "Be cool," he said. "Good luck."

Yo-Yo called out, "Use your tokens, folks. Don't pay to get busted for sneakin' in." He was in fine form.

They left, grins fixed on their faces.

Hall turned to the second group of youngsters. "You people have five minutes." He noted the time on his pad and motioned Goldenson and Wendy to study the map with him. "This is the cage," he said. "This is the place we hope to catch the rat." He pointed to the One hundred and thirty-seventh Street station, just a few blocks from where they were located. "The first group starts at Ninety-sixth, the second at One hundred and sixty-eighth. At exactly the same time, if we do it right, we all converge on One-thirty-seventh. We catch the fucker in the middle—if there is a fucker there."

They stood beside each other and looked at the map, though at this moment there was little to see. The plan was simple and obvious: the groups would start outside the area where the cardboard scraps had been found and converge in the hope of trapping the killer between them. If they could manage it properly, if they could keep him moving without alarming him, then there was a chance that it would work. If they could coax him into the right blind alley then there was a chance that they might catch him there. But it all assumed, of course, that he was hiding somewhere in the maze . . . that Goldenson was right, as he had been so far. . . .

Hall checked his watch again and nodded to Simba, the leader of the second group. Five more youngsters moved quickly out the door. The joking was noticeably absent.

Hall turned to the last two youngsters, Yo-Yo and another boy, clearly the smallest and youngest in the gang. "You two go on ahead, we'll meet you at the station. You know what he looks like now, so if he comes out in the open you can spot him. Just keep your eyes open. If you see him, stay out of the way. If he goes into the street, you both follow him. You go where he goes, you watch what he does, and then one of you comes back and tells us where he's at. We'll be at the station in a little while."

They both nodded and left the room together. Even Yo-Yo looked tense.

Hall turned to Wendy, showing more of his true feelings now that the boys were gone. "It's getting crazier and crazier," he said. "We don't even know the real enemy for certain. We have a picture of someone who's done something, but I'm still not convinced he's the one we should be after. . . ." He looked at Goldenson without apology.

"The man in that flier damn well has done *something*," Wendy said. "We know that for *sure*. He's killed hundreds of people. He has the ability to kill thousands more." She strained to make her argument clear, as precise as possible. "Every single thing we know suggests he'll try again. The Irving did in our enclosure . . . he never gave up until it was all over." She took Goldenson by the hand. "Let's not forget that simple fact. Let's not get sidetracked by all the other craziness." She looked at the photograph again. "We may all have our fantasies. We know we all can do crazy things. But none of us has done what this bastard has done. Not even close. Not even my brother— not yet. And there's nothing to prove that any of us would ever do what this Irving has done." She turned to Goldenson again and squeezed his hand. "I don't believe any of us ever would. There does happen to be a difference between the fantasy and the act."

Hall nodded. Her words had had their intended effect. At least for now he agreed that they were on the right course. "Okay, let's get it going and see what turns up," he said. He was still with them.

With Wendy in the middle and Hall and Goldenson on either side they walked the short distance to the One hundred and thirty-seventh Street subway station. The morning sun shone brightly now and the neighborhood was fully awake. Children were out of their hot apartments, already in the streets, waiting for the fire hydrants to be turned on so they could splash and play in the water. Addicts and alcoholics were in front of the buildings, resting on the stoops, taking the warmth of the sun into their decimated bodies, making provocative remarks to the mothers who pushed baby carriages to day care centers and then rushed off to the subways and to work.

The station was almost empty when the threesome arrived. Hall spoke with the man in the change booth. It was obvious that he had been informed of their activities. They entered through the exit door, not having to pay a fare. A train had just pulled out, heading downtown, and except for the two youths who had been sent ahead there was no one on the platform.

"Think he's a cop?" Hall asked.

"It would figure," Goldenson replied. "Better keep away from him."

The youngsters quickly approached. "Nothing happening," Yo-Yo said.

"No sign, no nothing," said the other boy.

A train pulled into the uptown side of the station, across the tracks. A small group of passengers disembarked, mostly old women returning to Harlem after nights spent as nurses aides or as cleaning ladies in deserted office buildings. They were the ex-wives and mothers of the men on the stoops.

"Nothing across there," the second youngster said. "Hardly anyone gets off. All the action is on the downtown side. All the people are going to work."

"We have to cover it anyway," said Hall. He checked his watch. "If we flush him he won't be getting off a train, he'll be on the tracks. We can't assume anything. We can't leave him a hole to escape through." He spoke to Yo-Yo: "You get over there now. I'll join you in a little while. We still have plenty of time."

It was a shock to see him jump down. In all their years of riding subways Goldenson and Wendy had never seen someone violate the rule that kept one on the platform. Now they watched with more than a little fear as Yo-Yo picked his way slowly and carefully across the four rows of tracks, two for local trains and two for express, that went through the station. They saw him cock his head, look down the track, and step beside a pillar. For a moment, until they heard the train, they thought he'd seen something. Then the express plummeted through the station, traveling very fast, and for the few seconds that it was visible they could see that it was full of passengers, the tail end of the rush hour, whites from the northern tip of Manhattan, some perhaps from Riverdale, still on their way to work.

Then the train was gone, leaving only a little cool air in its wake, and Yo-Yo finished his trip to the other side. He appeared to be completely relaxed. He pulled himself easily onto the platform and waved that all was well. Then he positioned himself on a bench where he could observe both the tracks and the passengers who left the train. It was hard to imagine how he could stop the large man they had seen in the photograph, but there he was anyway, committed to the job they'd assigned him.

Hall checked his watch. "They should get here in exactly an hour. They're supposed to hit the station at the same second. If they do flush him we'll have enough people on the scene to have a decent chance of grabbing him. All we have to do till then is sit and keep our eyes open. We've agreed that if we spot him, we don't move on our own. We try to slow him down, distract him, keep him busy until we get a group around him." He paused for a moment and glanced at Wendy and Goldenson and the youngster beside them. "You have any questions? I'll be right across the tracks, so we can all keep an eye on each other."

They nodded that they understood.

He looked at the youngster who was to remain on the platform with Wendy and Goldenson. "I think it would attract less attention if you kept your distance." He motioned with his head toward a bench down at the far end. "Why don't you act like you're nodding out." The youngster set off immediately, and Hall tapped Goldenson on the shoulder and jumped down on the track himself. "See you later."

They watched him make his way across the tracks. Some passengers had entered the platform now and they too watched his progress. Instead of spreading out across the platform to board a train at different doors they clustered together in silence near the turnstiles.

"Everyone's afraid of everything," Goldenson said to Wendy. "That's what we're reduced to."

She took his hand and held it tightly as they sat beside each other on the bench. "This thing has brought out the worst in all of us," she said.

'The worst, or the truth?" he asked.

"The worst."

The downtown local came slowly into the station. From where they sat they were able to observe the motorman as he manipulated his controls. He brought the train smoothly to a stop. They watched the conductor in his own small compartment press the button that opened the doors. Few people left the train. The group that had huddled together on the platform now spread out quickly and stepped aboard. The doors closed. Only Wendy, Goldenson and the youngster down at the other end remained on the platform. The train jerked forward. The conductor looked out of his window and stared impassively at them as the train picked up speed. Some of the passengers who had been on the platform, who were now leaning against the doors, also stared at them. For some unaccountable reason Goldenson broke into a smile. He waved. Then he froze when Wendy gasped. In the last car of the train, with his face pressed hard against the rear window, distorted and grotesque but still recognizable, he saw her brother. She clutched his hand, and they watched Francis disappear as the train plunged into the tunnel.

He tried to keep calm. "I thought he would be out of the way. I thought your father would have caught up with him by now."

She stayed silent. All he could feel was her pressure on his hand. "They can't do everything," she said. "They do have more important things than tracking down my brother—"

"There's nothing to worry about, he's probably just checking to see if we fell for his ploy."

"We don't really know why he's here," she said evenly. "For all we know it could be some kind of trap."

"Don't get carried away. You never thought he had it in him to be violent."

"Listen to trusting Solomon," she said. "One would think you'd know better."

Hall motioned to them from across the tracks. "What happened?" He formed the words silently.

Goldenson paused only a moment. "Her brother." His reply was silently mouthed. "On the train."

Hall shook his head, confused. The only clear thing to do was sit tight and wait for the others to get there. And so they sat there in silence, scrutinizing the passengers, peering up and down the tracks, seeing nothing remotely suspicious. Just another day on the New York subway.

Hall looked at his watch. He held up five fingers. They nodded, grew tense and continued to look up and down the tracks. Exactly five minutes later they saw the groups come into view. One youngster covered each track while one brought up the rear. They looked grimy and exhausted, but it was obvious that there had been no further sign. Hall motioned both groups in the direction of Wendy and Goldenson. He crossed the tracks again with Yo-Yo and they all gathered beside the bench.

"It's a nice clean subway track," Simba said. "No dirt, no people, no nothing. Safe as can be. Just a fat old rat every once in a while, a subway rat. Nothing to get uptight about, nothing this here cat can't handle."

Hall had been right about their persistence. They were down but not seriously discouraged. They would learn from the experience. The reward, if nothing else, was still a potent lure.

"You covered everything?" Hall asked.

"Every inch. Every tunnel. Every storeroom."

Both groups nodded agreement.

"You could walk it in half an hour," one boy said. "That's no problem, even with the trains. What slowed us down were the side trips. We broke a few locks. We found a place where some old rummy goes to drink. Then we had to hustle our asses. The tunnel is clean. Wherever that mother's hiding, he isn't here."

"We had the same thing coming down." Bullet was the leader of the group that had come from uptown. "The cat isn't here. He may have dropped that stuff, but he didn't stick around and he didn't drop anything else."

In the center of the platform, where another group of passengers waited, the man from the change booth ran into view. He immediately saw the gang and ran in their direction. "Something's happenin'," he said. "Midtown. It just come over the police radio. An A train's been stopped at Seventy-second. Central Park West. The Independent Line. They just sent out a general call. They need ambulances and reinforcements. He hit again, there could be a thousand people in that train. . . ."

Another train rolled into the station. It was heading downtown, in the direction of the disturbance, though not on the same line. Hall reacted instantly. "All right, let's get him."

They all followed him into the train. "Call the police," he said to the man before the doors began to close. "Let them know we're headed for Seventy-second," and they were on their way.

Wendy looked at Hall. "Do you think anybody really gives a damn where we're headed?"

Hall looked at her. "They will."

·35·

THE TRAIN RUMBLED downtown at a normal speed, with no indication that another disaster was in the making. The group followed Hall through the sliding door and across the open platform to the car ahead of them and through that car to the one ahead. When they got to the first car of the train the few passengers seated there withdrew from them in fear. They mistook them for a gang on the rampage.

"Take it easy, folks," said Hall, "no problem." He went directly to the subway map, which was partially obscured by graffiti. He strained to examine the part of the system he wanted to study. He motioned the others to take seats beside him. He looked at the map again, peering at it intently, trying to devise on the spot some kind of plan.

The train arrived at One hundred and twenty-fifth Street. As soon as the doors opened all the other passengers immediately left the car. They were taking no chances. The doors closed again on just the fifteen of them, they had the car to themselves. They were dirty and frightened, but also elated. They felt they were closing in and they felt ready. Irving was really there . . . no question. The train pulled out of the station.

"The motorman," Goldenson said. He walked to the front of the car. Through the window he could see track stretch into the distance. It was a sight he had loved as a little boy when he'd spent hours riding the subway, looking out of the window and imagining he was driving the train, in control. . . . He pounded

on the door to the motorman's booth. At first there was no answer, but after he pounded a second time the steel door opened
slightly.

"We're working with the police," he called out. "It's
okay. . . ."

The man glanced at him briefly, then turned away again to
look at the track in front of them.

"Did you hear about Seventy-second Street?"

Again the motorman glanced at Goldenson, skeptical.

"There's been trouble there."

"How the hell do you know?" He spoke without looking at
Goldenson. "What the hell kind of trouble?"

"The clerk at One thirty-seventh told us. A train's been attacked, held up."

"Jesus Christ," the man said. He slammed his door hard and
locked himself tight in his compartment, clearly now terrified
of Goldenson.

They began to slow for the next station, One hundred six-
teenth Street.

"He didn't know," Goldenson told the others. "Now he's
scared to death." And who wasn't?

The doors opened. Several passengers were about to enter.
Each looked at the group and chose instead to enter another
car. Everyone was jumpy, even without any knowledge of Seventy-second Street. They were still alone as the doors closed
again and the train continued downtown.

"Here's where it's at," said Hall. He motioned to the map
and they gathered around him. Graffiti covered the place
where he pointed, but the paint was thin and they could make
out the line beneath it. "We know he did something here." He
traced the subway line that the killer had struck. It was three
long blocks east of the Broadway Line, which they were riding,
and there were no connections between them until farther
downtown. "Our only chance is to get over to the Independent
Line and try to pin him down and grab him in the area he's in
now. We don't go right to that train because it's going to be a
disaster area. We figure him to be on the outskirts, watching
maybe, or in hiding, not in the middle of it. We have to trap
him." He made a pincer movement with his fingers. The plan
was a variation of the search they'd just completed. "Group A

gets off this train at Ninety-sixth Street, runs three blocks east to the Independent, gets down on the tracks at Central Park West, heads south in his direction. The rest of us stay on this train, go down to Fifty-ninth or even Fiftieth, and then head north. If we're lucky, if he's still in the area we nail our Irving in between."

"And if we're not lucky?" someone asked.

"He nails us."

They felt they at least had the jump. He'd struck in the subway. The "hunch" they had begun with—Goldenson's vision—had been correct. They were prepared for Irving . . . all of them thought of him by that name now, even if its unique meaning had special impact only for those who had shared the experience of the rat, and for them—especially Goldenson and Wendy—the link between the animal of the enclosure and the one secreted in the city's bowels was not only compellingly real, it was a though a merger, a fusion had now transcended mere connection. And, of course, for Goldenson, there was a private matter even Wendy could not fully share.

Yes, they were prepared for Irving. Hopefully it would take time for the police to mobilize, being busy as they undoubtedly must be with the victims. With luck the group would reach him before he was scared off, or captured by the police. And that last seemed almost more threatening than the former. Irving was theirs. For their various reasons, he belonged to them. He owed them. They meant to collect. . . .

The train pulled into the One hundred and third Street Station. The doors opened, closed. They were off again. The five members in A group prepared to leave. Hall patted each of them on the rear, as if they were starting a football game, and they all dashed out onto the platform when the train stopped at Ninety-sixth Street and the doors opened again.

Now two policemen entered the car. They eyed the remaining group but made no effort to interfere with them. They went at once to the front of the car and pounded on the motorman's door. He failed to respond, and they pounded again and again. Finally he did peek out, then pulled it open all the way when he saw their uniforms. One man stepped into the booth and began to talk. The other stood with his back to the window and eyed the passengers.

Wendy decided to approach him. The police were her territory.

He looked at her suspiciously. She could see that his face was flushed and that his hand hovered in the vicinity of his pistol. He seemed near panic.

"We know what's happening," she said quietly. "We're working with you."

He looked at her blankly.

"My father and brother are on the force," she said. "McGhie."

He gave no sign of recognition.

"Do you know how bad it is?" she asked.

"I can't talk to you, lady. The whole city's in an uproar. We're here to make sure this train gets where it's supposed to go."

"Has it been rerouted?" She was worried about their plan.

"You'll find out soon enough."

"Look, we're on the same side. You have to tell me." Desperation was in her voice.

"Lady, I don't have to tell you anything." He softened a bit. "Hell, I don't even know anything."

"Just tell me where we're going."

"Forty-second Street."

"Why there?"

"Don't ask me. I got an order and I'm carrying it out. I told you, I don't know what the hell is going on."

He would say nothing more and seemed so close to panic that she was afraid to push him. She returned to her seat beside the others as he continued to watch them. "Forty-second Street," she said.

They all looked out of the window as the train approached the Eighty-sixth Street Station. There was no sign that they were slowing down. If anything, their speed increased. The conductor gave three loud blasts of his horn and the passengers on the station jumped back in surprise and alarm. In seconds they were back in the tunnel, with the lights all green ahead of them. Their speed continued to increase. The train swayed and rattled as it hurtled along. They looked at the policeman and he looked stonily at them as the train shot downtown. They'd never traveled so fast in a subway before and wondered if the train could take the speed without jumping the track. They sped through the Seventy-ninth Street station with their horn again blaring. This time the platform was empty; the police must have cleared it of passengers. They were getting organized.

Now there was a sudden jolt, they all lurched forward, and the train moved slowly. They stood up and looked up ahead at what little they could see around the bulk of the policeman. There were yellow lights ahead. The train began to crawl. Now there were lights all around them. They pulled slowly into the Seventy-second Street station. Only three blocks away, in a tunnel due east of the one in which they were traveling, was the train that the killer had hit . . . and the cloud of parathion that he had released.

The Seventy-second Street station was total confusion. The police had not yet been able to control the crowd. People milled all about the platform. They knew that something serious was wrong, and though no one knew precisely what it was, they'd had enough experience to know by now that it must involve the killer. They too were dangerously close to panic.

"We have to get downtown," Hall said. "We'll never get to him from here."

The doors of their train opened onto the teeming platform. Crowds rushed in to fill the car.

"This train will take no passengers," said a voice on the loudspeaker. "This train will take no passengers . . ." But no one listened, no one paid any attention. Across the platform on the express track was another packed train. "That's the one that's going," the policeman said. "It's the last train out of here. All service stops after this . . ."

"We got to get into it," said Hall. He started out of their local with the others behind him and pushed his way to the door of the waiting express. It was jammed with bodies, people trying to get downtown, late for work, frightened, confused. There didn't appear to be any room at all, certainly not enough for the ten of them. Hall looked at Jumbo. He knew exactly what to do.

"Hey, you mothers, we got to get in here." Jumbo's eyes bulged and his face looked ferocious.

People immediately began to back away. Space appeared

172

where there had been none before. Passengers stepped out onto the platform. Better late than be cut, or worse.

They piled in, just in time before the doors closed suddenly. They'd all made it.

Goldenson, wedged between Wendy and the door, had been the last to enter the car and had tried to find a protected corner for himself. It didn't help. His nightmare had just come true. He was in the middle of the thing he had always feared, and he was sure he could never tolerate it, could never survive even the short ride they had ahead of them.

The train jerked forward. Very slowly, straining under the weight, it began to move.

"He's going to get us," Goldenson said, gasping.

Wendy looked at him and saw his terror. They were all clamped so tightly together that she could do nothing to comfort him.

The train stopped. They had scarcely moved. The walls of the tunnel around them were solid black. "We were so stupid." Goldenson looked at Hall. "We jumped like stupid rats. *You're* a stupid rat and we followed you. He has us exactly where he wants us. He set it up ... he's been waiting for us all the time...."

The train jerked forward again and now began to move at a steady pace. They could look out the window but all there was to see were the dirty walls and pillars and from time to time a feeble yellow light.

"We have to go back," Goldenson said. There were tears in his eyes. "Go back, he's going to get us...."

A woman who heard him began to cry. She believed him. Everyone strained to catch his words.

"*Cool* it." Hall edged backward and pressed himself against Goldenson, as much to control him as comfort him. His tone was harsh. "You just *cool* it. Shut your mouth. We got problems enough without you falling apart now...."

The train stopped again. The lights went out.

A piercing sound came from Goldenson that he neither willed nor recognized. Everyone backed away, even Wendy and Hall in the first shock of his panic. Only a dim emergency light illuminated the scene. Beneath it was the door at the end of the car. He immediately made for it, and the people that filled the aisle somehow got out of the way. He pushed and pulled his way to the space between the cars. Here at least there was air for him to breathe. He pulled himself up over the chains that enclosed the space. It felt a little better. He looked down at the track, at the glistening steel beneath him, and then at the tunnel around them. He saw in the dim light that there was space between the tunnel and the side of the train. Impulsively, without thought of the consequences of his act, he lifted himself over the gate and lowered his body down onto the ground beside the train.

He felt better immediately. His thoughts became more organized. He knew there was a third rail and if he touched it he would be electrocuted. He knew that the train might start at any moment and if he was in its path he would be killed. But none of this frightened him. None of it felt serious. None of it compared with the terror he felt inside the crowd. His emotion now was relief, though he was still too close to the terror to be clear even that he was feeling an emotion. He moved with intuition, like an athlete who must act without thinking, before the thought is formulated in his brain.

He walked slowly toward the front of the train. It was light enough for him to see his way, but too dark for the others to observe him. He had to be careful. It was as though he were passing by the body of a sleeping animal. He could feel its heat and hear its heavy breathing. One false move, one unnecessary sound and it would awaken and destroy him. He had to hide from it, protect himself from its destructiveness and from his own response. If it awakened, it they came after him, he might fight back.

Now he reached the front of the train. He could see the red lights stretching out into the distance, and realized that the train would stay where it was until the lights turned green. The train could not go through a red light even if the conductor attempted it. He looked back at the front of the train and could tell from the calls and shouts that they had seen him. They seemed so far away, as if in a dream, and old dream, one that he was at last escaping. He even smiled. It felt wonderful to be out of there, to be away from all of them, to be free. . . . He walked off slowly down the center of the track.

The train faded behind him. Everyone faded behind him.

Goldenson gave no thought to his actions. It was unnecessary. He was dimly aware of shouting, dimly aware that a bag containing a gas mask and a flashlight was still draped across his shoulder and that a knife was still in his pocket. It didn't seem to matter. What did was that he felt peaceful, relaxed, free of the mob at last, as if he finally had reached the place in life where he was meant to be.

He walked two hundred yards down the track. It was a complex part of the subway system where many tracks intersected and branched off in new directions, where trains from different lines ran beside each other, sometimes on the same level, sometimes one above the other. He couldn't have chosen a more strategic location. The train had stopped where all the lines converged. He was at the center of it all. He was the last one, alone, finally alone. The world was out of the picture. He was a creature unto himself who no one could disappoint, nothing could hurt. . . .

Noise broke through, brought him back from his special place. Something was coming, something was coming to crowd him. Something was coming to destroy the peace he'd just found. He reached for the knife in his pocket and withdrew it silently. He moved behind a pillar and waited. Something crossed an adjacent track. It was a large figure dressed in black. It carried a pack on its back and it strained under the weight. He knew at once who it was. He felt he'd known it all his life without benefit of photographs. He watched in terror, and in fascination. It started down the track. It seemed to know exactly where it wanted to go. The waiting train was its destination. Its pack contained its weapon. It approached a signal light and crouched beside the control box. It had caused the train to stop and could see it now. It had set it up that way. Now it appeared it would change the signal and cause the train to move.

Goldenson observed it . . . him . . . the man. He felt almost immobilized, as when he'd first been struck with the significance of Irving in the enclosure.

But his reverie was broken by the memory, and then the jolting awareness of the moment's reality, and the threat to Wendy. . . . He watched the man work on the signal. Goldenson held his knife tightly in his hand. The sound, he realized, would echo if he pressed the button. The click would alert *him*. He

175

was unable to move . . . almost didn't want to move. He didn't know which way to move. . . . The light turned green. All the way down the track the lights turned green. What was the noise he heard? Had the train already started?

Goldenson still hesitated. The noise in the distance increased in intensity. It was not a train but the sound of people. They were coming after him . . . after the two of them . . . maybe Wendy would be among them, maybe Hall. . . . Irving would destroy them unless he got Irving first. . . . He pressed the button. The blade clicked open. Loud as a gun shot.

It turned, leapt to its feet with all the grace Irving had once shown. It . . . he, dropped his screw driver, which bounced off the track. Now he held the nozzle of a hose. They were twenty yards apart. Goldenson's knife was useless. Their eyes met. The man looked so young, handsome, more alive than in his photograph.

"You can't get away with this," Goldenson said, feeling almost foolish with the banal words, and terrified by the indescribable act the words so weakly referred to.

The man was silent. His eyes burned into Goldenson. It seemed almost sexual. Horribly familiar.

"They have you surrounded. They know your name."

The man cocked his head, at first as though confused, then alertly listened to the approaching sound.

"If you surrender now you can stay alive," Goldenson said, realizing that in his terror he was talking nonsense, as though Irving were some ordinary criminal to be talked sense to. He felt worse than in the subway car.

The man merely looked at him.

"You can give your *reasons*." Goldenson would try anything. His only hope, he felt, was to stall. "You've planned it all, you must have thought about it, you have a reason, you have something to say . . ."

At first the man made no response. His eyes were still on Goldenson. "You know the reason," he said finally. It was such an ordinary voice. The shock of hearing it shattered him.

They both heard voices in the tunnel. Coming closer.

Someone shouted. It was from Hall's group. They were in sight but still too far away.

A squealing sound. A large brown rat came up the track, the

same kind that Yo-Yo had noted earlier. It brushed the man and darted past Goldenson. For the first time the man looked humanly frightened. His poise was shaken. More squealing, and he turned involuntarily.

"They're coming for *you*," Goldenson shouted.

Hall's gang had alarmed a community of rats, and now a squealing pack approached. The man tried to back away, there was nowhere to go. He pulled the trigger on his hose. Parathion sprayed in all directions. Rats commenced to die around him. He was the center of a cloud of poison. Nothing could come close. Goldenson ran back the other way. He pulled on his mask. The man became more agitated. He was breathing his own fumes. He tried to let go of the hose, tried to turn it off but found he was unable to do so. His fingers refused to obey. His hand shook violently. His clothes were soaked. His arm struck a pillar and the hose slipped away. Suddenly the spray stopped but it was too late. Dead rats littered the track. The man had breathed more than enough to kill himself. Goldenson watched him stagger. He was unable to maintain his balance. He thrust his hands out in different directions. He crashed into a pillar, out of control. He fell to the ground, began to convulse. A leg shot out and touched the third rail. The convulsions intensified—a combination of poison and electricity. Sparks sprayed the air. His body flailed. The leg finally came free. He lay there, motionless.

·36·

THEY WALKED UP the tracks toward the station, with Hall and the kids congratulating each other, slapping palms and backs and butts, and Goldenson off by himself, trailing behind them, quiet. He shared none of their elation. Irving was dead, but for Goldenson the terror of Irving was hardly over.

"Hey man, look here," one of the boys called out. Beside the track, between two pillars, was an air compressor and a container of liquid. It appeared ready to be activated. All that remained was for someone to flip the switch.

"The son of a bitch had a regular old-fashioned ambush going," Hall said. "All he needed was another train in the right place. He was trying to hit the whole damn system—"

"That mother hits *nothing* anymore. He's had his lunch."

"It's our turn, baby! We gonna get that money and we gonna fly!"

Goldenson listened to them. It was as if he was under water. He heard them clearly, was aware of their excitement, understood it, even empathized with it, yet found that he felt none of it. He knelt down beside the apparatus, as if to examine it, and stared at the switch. He felt it pull at him. He had only to touch it. No one would have time to use his mask, he could destroy himself and the others in the process. No one would ever know . . . the police would assume they'd walked into a trap. He hovered there for a moment . . . then backed away. And now he had another impulse, to pull the plug and deactivate the equipment. He restrained that one too . . . after all, he told himself, nothing should be touched until the police arrived. Was that really his reason . . . or his excuse?

"We really did it," Hall said. He put his arm on Goldenson's shoulder. "I can't believe it."

"I can't believe anything." Goldenson hardly knew what he was saying. He stepped away from Hall. All he cared about now was getting out of the tunnel as soon as possible, getting back to Wendy. . . .

Hall stayed beside him. He treated Goldenson with a tenderness that had never been in their relationship before. It was clear how much he needed it, how upset he really was. He placed his arm around him again and this time Goldenson allowed it to remain. "Almost," he said. "Just a little farther. We'll be out of here soon."

And they emerged that way from the tunnel. They blinked and looked dazed when they reached the station and came into the light. A train was standing empty on another track. The station had been closed. At the far end of the platform men and women in white uniforms were working frantically with the injured survivors of the first attack. The station had been turned into a makeshift hospital. At first no one noticed them. Finally a policeman turned. They waved. He put his hand on his gun, then called to another officer. The two of them ran down the platform.

"What's going on? Is there another train in there?"

"It's all over," Hall said.

"What's all over?"

"We got him."

The policemen were confused. They had no idea how to respond. They decided to help Hall and Goldenson onto the platform. They extended their hands and lifted each up.

"Got *who?*" one of the officers asked.

"Who else?" Hall said. "The guy who did all this." He extracted the photograph from his pocket in the hope that it would convince them.

A policeman pointed down the platform. The boys were climbing up from the track. "They with you?"

Hall nodded.

The policemen looked up the platform for a superior officer.

Finally one caught his sergeant's eye and called him in their direction. The gang members approached and stood quietly beside them. They were all standing there together when the first reporter saw them.

Within five minutes of the gang's emergence from the tunnel the police organized a crew and dispatched it to the place that Hall described. They brought coffee for Hall, Goldenson, and the boys. A doctor came to examine Goldenson and was unable to find any signs of illness. He returned quickly to the victims at the other end. Whatever was affecting Goldenson, what caused his speech to slur and his mind to work so slowly appeared not to be physical.

Finally Wendy and her father arrived. Goldenson immediately spotted her as she came down the stairs to the platform, and he ran over to her and took her in his arms.

"Is it over?" she asked. "Really over?" The tears were pouring from her as they held tight to each other. "My brother's gone," she said. "Francis . . . he got caught in the tunnel . . . they say he was trying to stop the killer . . . they're making him a hero. God knows why he was really there. . . ."

Lieutenant McGhie touched his shoulder. There were tears in his eyes as well. They shook hands. The three of them stood together for a moment without speaking. Then, finally, McGhie said, "You did a good thing. I respect you for it. We owe you everything." He turned away now, crying openly.

A police officer came back from the site of the killer's death. He spoke briefly with another officer. Additional men were dispatched, one carrying a folded stretcher.

Goldenson swayed on his feet.

"It's been a rough day," she said.

"For you too." It felt like the first words he had spoken in days. "How did you get here?"

"They finally started the train. Backwards. Back to Seventy-second. I got out and called my dad's office and found out he was here. I ran all the way. You wouldn't believe what it's like outside. The city is going wild. It's a panic. I never imagined anything could be like this. It's worse than it was when he hit downtown. Everyone is ready to kill everyone else. He touched a nerve in all of us, we've all gone crazy."

"Maybe that was the point," he said.

The dignitaries began to arrive. First the police commissioner, who conferred briefly with his staff and then came to congratulate Goldenson and the others. More reporters and photographers reached the scene; their flashbulbs added an eerie note. At one end of the station were the dead and injured, with more bodies being brought out all the time. At the other end, the day's heroes, and the politicians, and the reporters.

The mayor arrived. To be photographed with the boys. He made a prepared statement for the television cameras. ". . . One hundred thousand dollars," he said to Goldenson. "A great day's work."

Everyone rushed to the side of the platform. The men with the stretcher had returned. It was obvious that beneath the sheet there was a body. A shiny black shoe protruded.

·37·

First there was shock, numbness, disbelief. They had been afraid so long. Then a wave of joy swept through the city. It was if a war had ended, as if the Mets and Yankees, Rangers, Knicks, and Jets had won their championships on the same day. Everyone came outdoors. The streets were jammed with happy, smiling people. The parks were filled. Musicians came out of their apartments and played their instruments for appreciative crowds. People stood beside each other on the sidewalks and trusted each other for the first time in years. They had all survived together. They were able to look each other in the face and meet each other's eyes. There was happiness and love in the air. Strangers embraced openly. Neighbors who had lived beside each other for years without ever speaking now greeted each other like old and long-lost friends. Enemies forgot their quarrels. Husbands and wives forgave each other everything.

Even the muggers remained inactive. The city suddenly was safe, safer than it had been in twenty years. For a few ecstatic days people stopped their talk of how it no longer worked. The subways went back to normal and no one minded the fact that the fare was due to rise again. People forgot their fear of the next financial crisis, forgot the certainty of another budget cutback, another deterioration in their lives. At least they had their lives. The killer's death released a flood of buried optimism, and for a heady period everyone felt that the problems could be solved, that the environment could be made livable again, that the sludge and garbage would vanish from the beaches and that the rivers could be restored. All it would take was energy, a new sense of the possibilities of life, which was now abundantly available.

The weekend following the killer's death was marked by a huge "Festival of Life" in Central Park. A stage was erected in the Sheep Meadow, where the survivors of the West Village poisoning had been given emergency aid. People came by the hundreds of thousands from all parts of the city and suburbs to dance to the music of as many different bands as there were ethnic groups within the city. Everything from "soul" to Latin music to Polish polkas to waltzes to Israeli and Arab and Irish and Italian music was played there through the night, with no friction between any of the celebrants, and with many leaving the scene for brief or sometimes longer periods in the private corners of the park, where they made love without interference or embarrassment or fear of danger. Everyone was starved for contact, everyone needed love, and no one had time for precautions. Nine months from the day the killer died the hospitals would be filled again. This time not with injured subway riders, but with mothers and babies. The lives the killer had destroyed would be replaced a dozen times over.

The mayor spoke on television. Even the President taped a message of congratulations for the city and sympathy for the families of those who had been killed. There were celebrations around the country. The old cynicism, the old contempt for the city was completely gone. Everyone shared the joy.

Goldenson was deluged with requests for interviews. He simply refused. Under no circumstances would he discuss his work or any of the factors that led to his insight into the killer. He took his share of the reward and went into seclusion. He wanted nothing to do with any of them. It all fell into Hall's lap. He made an impressive figure in the interviews with his articulate, decisive manner. He gave full credit to Goldenson and the others, repeated over and over again that it was Goldenson's experiment, Goldenson's insight, but his disclaimers began to be ignored. It was he that increasingly was thought of as the hero. The media needed someone. The part played by the Black Angels was soon forgotten; no one was interested in a gang of hoodlums. The support given by the police was underplayed. The group received their reward and divided it in the way they had agreed, but Hall got the attention. At first he appeared to enjoy it. It did, after all, guarantee his future. He was deluged with offers from medical schools. But soon he grew tired of it. No one was really interested in the truth. No one was interested in changing the world that had created Irving. He finally drew the line when he was offered a movie contract, and soon he stopped speaking to reporters at all.

Now speculation about the killer became the focus. The psychiatrists and social scientists came out of the woodwork. They pored over every bit of data available on the man. They dissected him in a way that Goldenson had never attempted. There were those who put the cause of his behavior in his environment. They talked about the pressures on people living in crowded cities, about the quality of life in a technological society, about the effects of violence on television, and even about the effects of the Vietnam war and the bombing on people who in one way or another, directly or on the tube, had participated in them. They eventually were dismissed. They found, like Hall, that no one was interested. Everyone had heard the same arguments for years. It was just too dull.

What caught the country's attention was Irving's personal history. One psychiatrist after another, one psychologist after another, stepped in front of the cameras to express an opinion on his life story. Each attempted in another plausible way to describe the factors that led him to act in his bizarre and destructive manner. Each used Irving's case history to validate his own approach, and each in his own way was correct. Irving was seen as an aberration; his behavior an aberration. It was a peculiar and unfortunate juxtaposition of life history and technological expertise. A spokesman from the Pentagon announced that new psychological screening procedures, based on personality tests of Irving during the time he served, had been devised. They would, in the future, exclude people with his pattern from the kind of training he received. The CIA said nothing.

Time passed. The weather changed. The football season started. The psychiatrists became too abstract. They talked less of Irving's sexual practices and more about his relationship with authority. Whether he was motivated by the Freudian "death instinct" became their preoccupation. The interviews grew dull. Everyone had had enough. There seemed nothing new to say. Even the few comedians who'd attempted to joke about Irving soon gave it up: their audiences were bored. Whatever the reason—whether a need to push the reality into the unconscious or a need to be stimulated by something new— within a month the event had disappeared from the thoughts of nearly everyone. Life went on. The muggers went back into action. The women who had been impregnated missed their first period. Some were happy. Some had abortions.

·38·

GOLDENSON LIVED through the weeks following the killer's death in a kind of fog. He saw no one but Wendy. He never returned to the college, never tried to organize his data, never communicated with the faculty committee that supervised his work. That part of his life was over, as empty as the enclosure, and he told himself he would never touch it again. He spent his time at Wendy's apartment, much of it with a stack of books on organic agriculture, and when he did go outside it was mostly to visit stores that specialized in camping and gardening equipment. All the methodical energy he had once lavished on his animals now poured into a plan for escaping the city. He and Wendy had finally agreed to try life on a farm. After much deliberation and research they chose an area in northern Ontario. While not as isolated as Alaska, its current and future conditions were more predictable, less vulnerable to the exploitation that was already destroying Alaska. He had been to that part of Canada on a canoe trip, and had always loved it.

Money was no problem. They bought equipment, seeds and a Volkswagen bus. They located a real estate broker in Ottawa who sent them descriptions of abandoned farms. One sounded ideal. Though it was closer to civilization than they had hoped —thirty miles on an old dirt road to the nearest town—they paid the small fee for the rental and purchase option. It was worth a try. They would learn what they could and go deeper into the woods next year if that was necessary.

Once the farm was chosen they moved quickly. Winter was not far off and they wanted to be settled in before snow made the house inaccessible. They knew it was risky, might be a disaster, but they would take their chances. It was a lesser risk than what they had lived through in the city.

When they were ready with a supply of tools and clothes and books and everything else on Goldenson's interminable list, they left the city. There was a last goodbye with Hall, and then on the way north another goodbye with her father and James in the Bronx. Goldenson sat outside in the loaded bus. Lieutenant McGhie came out to shake his hand, with James beside him. Then they were off on the Thruway north, the bus chugging along, slowly but valiantly, and the Catskill Mountains looking dark and beautiful as the sun went down.

When the sun came up they were in Canada, with the leaves already gold and the air already cool and the heater already inadequate. They met the real estate man in Ottawa, who gave them a surprised but friendly welcome, and a warning about the weather. He provided them with a detailed map, and the next day, after they'd stocked the bus with three hundred pounds of food, enough to last the winter and then some, they were on their way. After another day's drive north and west on paved roads they spent the night in a clearing, in their sleeping bags, looking up at the cold, crystal sky. No passing automobiles disturbed their sleep. At dawn they ate a cold breakfast and set out again amidst the crimson and yellow trees with a sense of the vast deserted land around them. The pavement ended, more or less abruptly, in an impoverished village which they fled almost at once, after filling the tank with gas.

Now the going became slow and difficult. The dirt road was narrow and rutted. Their average speed was under ten miles an hour and the overloaded bus swayed and bumped precariously, threatening at any moment to break a spring or axle. Every few miles they passed what appeared to be an abandoned farm. Once, exactly where it was indicated on the map, they skirted the shoreline of a small lake that had not a single building on it. He reached out and touched her hand and they stopped there briefly for a drink of water. The lake was clean and pure.

"We can get fish here," he said. "Even in winter. I brought a tool to cut through ice. We'll always have fresh bass. In the spring we'll get lake trout. It's a great source of protein."

They wobbled along the road and were scraped by the branches of the overhanging trees and rocked by the ruts and stones along their way. In places it seemed more like a dried stream bed than a road constructed by man, and it was at just those places that he felt the deepest pleasure and relief.

"It would take two days to walk out of here," she said. "Two good days. Maybe three after it snows."

"Let's hope we don't have to," he said.

"We won't have to. I'm just figuring."

At last they reached the farm. Perhaps all that could be said was that once, years ago, it had been a kind of farm, though hardly one that had ever been productive. More recently it had been a hunting camp. There was an overgrown field and a white, peeling building, a good fifty years old, with a sagging porch and a rusted screen door. Miraculously, the windows were intact, a good sign and a striking contrast with the city that seemed already so far away. Behind the house, beside the field, were three barren apple trees, and on a branch of one hung an old, weathered but still functional swing. It was another good sign, and Wendy ran to it, sat on it, and smiled when she found that the rope held her. She kicked herself into motion as he stood there watching, in the place where he wanted to be at last, in the cool autumn air that smelled of grass and leaves and came to them directly from the unpopulated forests to the north.

The branch creaked and she left the swing and they walked together slowly, arm in arm, around the house. They came to the outhouse, and he inspected it. "It smells sweet," he said. "No one's used it for a long time."

"It'll smell sweet after we use it," she said, and she kissed his neck. She ran out into the field. It was heavily overgrown, but the cold weather had thinned it back. She danced there, under the blue sky, in the warm sun, the first time she had ever danced for him.

"Let's look inside," he said when she had finished, after they'd embraced again.

The lock worked, but the door was stuck tight. They had to

push together to force it open, and the hinges squeaked as it yielded. Inside it smelled musty, but there was less dust and damage than they had expected. It was as if the dirt and destructiveness they both took for granted as part of their lives in the city was simply gone. Things aged differently. They deteriorated less, and when they did finally deteriorate there was always some redeeming feature, some beauty the process revealed that made it acceptable.

They stepped into the living room. The mirror was intact on the wall. Animals had nested in the couch and droppings were scattered around the floor.

"Field mice," he said. "No Irvings."

She stood beside him. "We can make it here," he said. "We'll be all right."

Later they cleared and swept the living room. Reluctantly, they decided the couch was beyond salvation. They dragged it outside and left it on the porch. He drove the bus in close to the house and unloaded their supplies. He arranged everything as neatly as possible. They worked for several hours, and when they were finished it was all there in front of them on the living room floor, the equipment and food and weapons they hoped would get them through the winter. It didn't look like very much.

"For the next two weeks we'll be cutting wood," he said.

"We'll be all right," she said. "I know it in my bones."

The days went by, flowing one into the other, filled with unending work and crowned with idyllic lovemaking. The pile of wood outside the door grew steadily, though most days now a curl of smoke could be seen drifting from the chimney. The air was cold in the morning, often below freezing, but the days were sunny and mild and they had time to complete their tasks. The inside of the house took shape, cheerful and serviceable, sealed against the winter they knew was not far off. They visited the town and bought a goat. They filled the bus with feed and repaired the barn for her. After some misgivings, and debate, they chose to name her Irving.

It was all so perfect and yet the memory of what they had escaped was still with them, hovering on the edges of their thoughts. At least once a week he awakened in the middle of the night in the middle of a scream. He would drip with sweat despite the chill. All she could do was hold him when he allowed her. She knew from experience it helped if they made love, but the dreams continued. He tried to shrug them off with an occasional joke about the goat. He said they had to keep their eye on her; she might live up to her name; they would have to watch her with the lamb they expected from her in the spring.

Once she found him face to face with a live field mouse in the kitchen. She walked in and saw him standing there, a broom in his hand and the mouse in a corner, unable to kill it though it had been stealing precious food. Her arrival broke the spell, and he promptly swung and killed it with a single blow and then lifted it by the tail and carried it into the woods. When he returned to the house she could see he was still upset.

"You had no choice," she said. "You know he was into the rice." She put her hand to her mouth, they looked at each other, and finally laughed, though a bit nervously.

"Well, it was him or us," he said, and smiled. He didn't feel especially amused.

But mostly there were the joyous moments: their hikes in the woods, his knowledge of mushrooms. Once they found a pine grove full of Boletus mushrooms and were able to gather huge quantities of them, some to eat that night and the rest to tie on strings and hang over the stove to dry. There was their trip back to the lake, where with the fishing rod he'd brought they quickly caught enough small-mouth bass for a glorious meal. He promised that when there was snow on the ground and they could better store the fish they would return and take a really large supply.

He was constantly preoccupied with their supply of food. Every few days he would weigh and measure everything they had on hand. He calculated, over and over again, that they had enough. He would not have to shoot a deer. His initial figures were correct, they could last the winter, but he was never satisfied and he had to check as often as possible. "Just like a rat," he said one day. "I have the hoarding instinct." He smiled. But that night he had another bad dream.

At last the snow began to fall. The first few times it barely dusted the frozen ground, but one day it really stormed and they knew from that day on they would not see bare earth again until the spring. There was less and less for them to do. The house was warm and tight. There was enough wood. They took to reading and painting and making love even more often. He made wood carvings. From time to time they listened to the radio, but the reception was poor, the Canadian stations uninteresting, and he was always pressing her to conserve the batteries.

They did occasionally listen to the news . . . their sole link to the outside world. It was on a Sunday that they heard about a hundred people killed in Mexico City. It seemed that someone had tampered with a railroad signal and caused a terrible crash. They listened more frequently after that. A week later some five hundred died when a gas main exploded in Tokyo. A mild earthquake was claimed to have been the cause. They were afraid they knew better. A day after that an elevator cable snapped in the Eiffel Tower, leaving fifty dead, and in Mexico City again, three hundred people died of contaminated grain. . . .

It was, of course, another Irving. Irvings.

And that night they made love as though there was no tomorrow.

THE BIG BESTSELLERS
ARE AVON BOOKS

☐	**Oliver's Story** Erich Segal	36343	$1.95
☐	**Snowblind** Robert Sabbag	36947	$1.95
☐	**Voyage** Sterling Hayden	37200	$2.50
☐	**Lady Oracle** Margaret Atwood	35444	$1.95
☐	**Humboldt's Gift** Saul Bellow	29447	$1.95
☐	**Mindbridge** Joe Haldeman	33605	$1.95
☐	**Polonaise** Piers Paul Read	33894	$1.95
☐	**A Fringe of Leaves** Patrick White	36160	$1.95
☐	**Founder's Praise** Joanne Greenberg	34702	$1.95
☐	**To Jerusalem and Back** Saul Bellow	33472	$1.95
☐	**A Sea-Change** Lois Gould	33704	$1.95
☐	**The Moon Lamp** Mark Smith	32698	$1.75
☐	**The Surface of Earth** Reynolds Price	29306	$1.95
☐	**The Monkey Wrench Gang** Edward Abbey	30114	$1.95
☐	**Beyond the Bedroom Wall** Larry Woiwode	29454	$1.95
☐	**Jonathan Livingston Seagull** Richard Bach	34777	$1.75
☐	**Working** Studs Terkel	34660	$2.50
☐	**Something More** Catherine Marshall	27631	$1.75
☐	**Shardik** Richard Adams	27359	$1.95
☐	**Anya** Susan Fromberg Schaeffer	25262	$1.95
☐	**The Bermuda Triangle** Charles Berlitz	25254	$1.95
☐	**Watership Down** Richard Adams	19810	$2.25

Available at better bookstores everywhere, or order direct from the publisher.